MW01141219

Sex and Sexuality

Willa Okati

A Samhain Publishing, Ltd. publication.

Samhain Publishing, Ltd.
512 Forest Lake Drive
Warner Robins, GA 31093
www.samhainpublishing.com

Sex and Sexuality
Copyright © 2007 by Willa Okati
Print ISBN: 1-59998-641-8
Digital ISBN: 1-59998-176-9

Editing by Sasha Knight
Cover by Anne Cain

This book is a work of fiction. The names, characters, places, and incidents are products of the writer's imagination or have been used fictitiously and are not to be construed as real. Any resemblance to persons, living or dead, actual events, locale or organizations is entirely coincidental.

All Rights Are Reserved. No part of this book may be used or reproduced in any manner whatsoever without written permission, except in the case of brief quotations embodied in critical articles and reviews.

First Samhain Publishing, Ltd. electronic publication: March 2007
First Samhain Publishing, Ltd. print publication: September 2007

Dedication

To the fine folks at my local Starbucks, purveyors of fine mocha lattes that keep a writer going through the night.

Chapter One

"There, look at you. Aren't you gorgeous?"

With both eyes closed, Quinn tilted his chin up. "Am I ready?"

"Almost." The gentle fingers expertly applying his makeup danced across his cheek. "I think we should have some glitter, right across those nice bones. You'll shine under the dance floor lights."

Quinn quivered in anticipation. "This club is everything you promised?"

"Sugar, it's beyond your wildest dreams." A brush feathered over Quinn's cheekbones, anointing him with what felt like the lightest dusting of powder. "Men stand in line for *ages* trying to get inside, but with these VIP passes they'll lower the ropes for us faster than you can get your pants down. And we all know how quick that can happen."

Quinn giggled. "Only when I'm really motivated." He snagged the wrist of the hand doing his makeup. "Your touch is just too much. How about we take the edge off right now?"

"Oh, tempting, tempting. But that sweet mouth is perfectly done. Wouldn't want you to spoil it before your big debut."

"Lipstick can always be fixed." Quinn opened up to gaze at the pert, pretty boy poised in front of him. He licked at the tangerine-flavored gloss on his mouth. "Stand up. Unfasten your jeans."

"Aren't you in a hurry?" The boy did as he was told despite his joking complaint.

"Mmm. When it comes to loving, there's no time like the present." Quinn drew the boy's cock out of his pants and licked a long stripe down one thick vein on his developing erection. "You taste wonderful."

CRAGEO

Quinn—no, Quentin—shifted in his uncomfortable plastic seat. The room he sat in was cold, no forced heat to warm his bones. But denying creature comforts was part of the Center's program.

"That's all I remember," he lied. "I guess what came afterwards was what always happened."

"And what was that?"

Quentin squirmed. "I...I used my mouth on his... We had sex," he confessed. "I couldn't resist the urge."

"A chief trait of sinners is being unable to resist temptation." The gray-bearded counselor Quentin was speaking to inclined his head as he imparted this wisdom.

Quentin kept silent, accepting the blame for what he'd done. These men and women in the Sainted Lady Rehabilitation Center were showing him the way. And he needed to learn. He wanted it.

His life had to change.

He snuck a peek at the man he spoke to. The advisor in his morning session had proved to be a blessing, as such things went. This was Father Andrew, a man who'd shown kindness to

Quentin in the past. Father Andrew wouldn't order him to be dunked in a steel tub full of ice cubes or scrubbed with a stiff brush to rid his flesh of its taint. Quentin always felt a sense of relief when he was talking to Father Andrew.

Although he knew better than to expect absolutely no punishment.

Silver-headed at the age of about fifty, Father Andrew wore the collar of a priest and the demeanor of a confessor, listening patiently but calculating up how much penance a man would have to pay for his sins. And he would exact that absolution down to the last drop.

"You realize now that you were in the wrong?" Father Andrew asked, patient as if they had all day. For all Quentin knew, they did. "The weakness of the flesh is common among our human race, but a man desiring the flesh of another man is both forbidden and contemptible."

"I do realize." Quentin gripped the edges of his seat. He bowed his head. "I want to change."

"You're here of your own free will," Father Andrew conceded. "There may be hope for you, Quentin. We'll get you back on the path of righteousness. You'll see."

CRICSSO

"Quentin? Professor Whiteside?" A hand slapped Quentin's shoulders. "Where were you?"

"What?" Quentin blinked. "I'm sorry. Woolgathering."

"Well, back to the present with you. You were falling behind."

"Of course." Quentin fell into step behind the two men taking him on a tour of Sweetwater College, the campus where he'd been lucky enough to secure a position.

He had to keep this position, this chance to prove himself. He'd come so far that he couldn't fail now. Time he refreshed his memory about the rules he'd learned at the Center and walked the straight and narrow again.

And those rules said, very clearly, no ogling men's asses. At the very least.

God. Was he that weak? After all he'd been through...

Quentin tried to distract himself by drinking in the scenery. Oh, but it was a gorgeous day. One could almost forget their problems here, in the foothills of Appalachia.

One could start fresh, if one wanted to.

"I'm glad you had the time to take a stroll," the tall man walking in front of Quentin said. "Wonderful place, isn't this?"

Quentin glanced around himself, taking in the leafy green trees and artfully casual botanical gardens as if it were the first time he'd seen them. Not so far from the truth. Every time he came up into the Gardens, he felt a mild sense of shock, as if he'd suddenly been transplanted from a smoggy, population-choked metropolis into Eden.

A new day, a new vista, a new life. Second chances. He wouldn't tangle up the clean lines of his life again. No more mistakes, no more looking where he shouldn't...

Speaking of which, he turned his eyes to the side, deliberately facing away from the tempting backside walking just a few steps in front of him.

He couldn't think like that anymore. He wasn't "that way". He'd been through the training and come out with high honors.

And to prove it, didn't he have a serious girlfriend now, almost a fiancée?

Quentin knew he could do this. All he had to do was try hard enough.

"I think you'll like it here." Professor Ten Hawks, "call me Ben", pronounced, then took in a deep breath and looked around himself. Even though he winced with guilt over the observation, Quentin couldn't help thinking that while the view was spectacular, the man pointing it out made those rolling hills look dull. Ten Hawks was pure Cherokee, almost six feet four with cropped black hair and strongly muscled legs. For their outing, he'd dressed casually in a T-shirt and jeans as if he wasn't the Chancellor of an entire college.

Quentin, in his button-down Oxford shirt with a mousy gray tie, felt somehow overdressed. He stole a glance at the other professor wandering with them, a young man from the Mathematics department. He couldn't have been much older than Quentin himself, probably around thirty, although he appeared to be the kind who would never look his age. Andy seemed to have the same laid-back attitude as Ten Hawks, as if they could take all day on their walk in the Gardens.

As if they didn't have things to do.

Quentin straightened his tie. A nervous habit, but it gave him something to do with his hands. "Yes, sir," he responded dutifully. "I like it here already."

Could you sound more like a brown-noser? Work on your responses, Quentin.

Ten Hawks didn't seem to notice anything lame about Quentin's reply, too busy focusing on the view and the nature surrounding them. He patted his chest. "You could hardly tell we're only two miles away from the city. The world up here is a wonderful thing. There's nothing like being in the foothills. It's as close as you can get to nature unless you actually hike up into the mountains. Do you? Hike, that is?"

Ten Hawks turned to Quentin as if he expected an affirmative answer. Quentin made an expression of apology. He hadn't been on a mountain hike since the Center's forced marches over rough terrain, and while he'd understood the need to punish the body, the memories were not pleasant.

"Not really," Quentin demurred, and then, because that didn't seem like a suitable response, fibbed, "I'd enjoy going sometime. Does the faculty sponsor excursions into the hills?"

Ben—Ten Hawks—laughed. The exact same kind of gently reprimanding chuckle the deprogrammers had used when Quentin was trying his best but still failing. "Not exactly. We're what you might call 'understaffed' here. That would be, gentlemen, because we're also what you would call 'under-funded'. We can thank a grant for the new teaching positions that have opened up—but then again, you know that. Right, Professor Byrne—Andy?"

Andy grinned behind Ten Hawks' back. "You could say that," he drawled in the sexiest—*no*. Quentin tried not to focus on him, with his elfin good looks, but to pay attention to the Chancellor. Not hard to do. No matter how handsome Andy might be—*stop it, Quentin, stop it*—Ten Hawks' eyes were piercing enough to stop anyone in their tracks. Quentin felt as if he were being given a quiz. *Oh, dear.* Had Ten Hawks felt the weight of Quentin's gaze on portions of his anatomy where no normal, well-trained eyes should go?

"I'm grateful for the position," he said in his most neutral voice. Not too enthusiastic, not too flat. "I was pleased to find something so soon after I'd graduated the Ph.D. program. And to be recruited, no less."

"Eyes and ears everywhere." Ten Hawks tapped his temple. "We do have an excellent line into the grapevine. Your dissertation on Jane Austen was a thing of beauty. We're lucky to have you, Professor Whiteside."

Quentin tried a tentative olive branch. "Please, call me Quentin."

"Quentin, then. Sorry. Foolish of me to forget. But it's good that you're informal. We like things a bit relaxed here. Work hard, but be true to yourself." Ten Hawks paused for a moment. "I'd like for you to keep that in mind when you meet your new roommate."

Quentin tilted his head slightly to the side. "I'd meant to ask you about him. I'd thought we were to report in yesterday, but the professor I'm sharing housing with still wasn't here this morning."

"Ah, yes." Ten Hawks puffed his cheeks out thoughtfully. "Billy Jennings. Wonderful work in American Literature, but definitely best described as unorthodox. He phoned me last night to warn me that he was running late."

Quinn kept his expression politely interested out of long habit. Inside, though, he felt his stomach roll. He'd been thrilled at the thought of living on campus for a fraction of what he'd pay for an apartment, less excited about the idea of sharing rooms, and now downright dismayed with the notion of a man who wasn't going to be...compatible.

He liked things orderly. Had to have them that way. In a line, on time, reliable and dependable. "Unorthodox" didn't fit in with his life as he'd planned it. "Unorthodox" would have his almost-fiancée Melissa in a snit when she came to visit.

How bad could it be, though?

"I'm sure we'll get along just fine," he said, keeping his voice pleasant. "When will I first need to meet with students? Do they begin arriving tomorrow?"

"Some will. Right now, the best thing you can do is get settled. Didn't you say the moving van was coming with your things around eleven?" Ten Hawks checked his watch. "You'll have just enough time to get back to the housing before they arrive."

Quentin nodded. He fought back the urge to tuck his hands in his pockets or, equally tempting, cross his arms over his chest. "I didn't want to run away before you were finished," he offered up apologetically. *Run away—oh, I shouldn't have said that.* "Should I leave?"

"You'd better, if you want the movers to know they're in the right place." Ten Hawks chuckled. "Go on, now. I don't need a chaperone. Been walking these gardens for ten years and counting. Just follow the trail until you see the sign for housing, and take a left. You'll be back in no time."

Andy gave Quentin a small nudge. Quentin stiffened, but managed to avoid pulling away. It wasn't a sensual touch. The mathematics professor didn't mean any harm. "How about I walk you back?" Andy suggested. "It's easier to get lost than Ben thinks. He knows this place like the back of his hand, but the rest of us? Not so much. Come on, it's this way."

Quentin cast a dubious look at Ten Hawks, but the tall Native American had already turned away and was sauntering down the path just as if he didn't have late professors, arriving students and a new semester almost ready to begin. "He's an interesting man," Quentin said carefully. "I have to wonder what he would call unorthodox."

"Ten Hawks? They'd have to go a ways for him to start throwing stones," Andy finished up with a grin. "I've heard a few things about Billy Jennings. You're gonna be in for a few speed bumps before you two settle in together, but I think it'll work out. Things usually do." He winked. "Let's get started. I'm heading for breakfast once I've dropped you off. I could cook, sure, but I suck in the kitchen. The cafeteria's not bad." He paused. "Do you want to go with me? They make a mean waffle. Defrosted and everything."

Quentin felt the man's gaze wandering over him, almost as if he were speculating on something. *No, no. Don't.* His cheeks colored as he shook his head. "It's all right," he heard himself say. "Why don't you go on ahead? I can find my way back just fine. I'm good at memorizing things. I should be all right getting back alone."

"You sure?" Andy seemed doubtful. "I mean, I don't mind."

"It's fine." Quentin made himself smile. Andy was harmless. He had to be for Ten Hawks to trust him, and he couldn't be offering anything more than a friendly hand. Probably. All the same, Quentin thought he'd feel better if he walked back alone. "Trust me."

Those two words usually had the desired effect. Andy's frown broadened into an easy grin. "Your call. I'll take a right when you take a left, then. See you around?"

"Of course." Quentin agreed cautiously. "We'll run into each other sooner or later."

"That's a fact. Sweetwater's nice, but God, is it small. Eight hundred students and twenty professors. This place wouldn't be running if Ten Hawks weren't in charge." Andy patted him on the back. "Later, friend."

Quentin watched as the mathematics professor started loping away down the right fork of the track. "See you around," he said, wincing at the lameness of his reply. He watched as Andy threw up a hand in a backwards wave, and couldn't help but look down the length of the man's body—the straight line of his back, his long legs, his firm, round a—

No. I'm not looking anymore. Not again. I have Melissa.

I'm walking on the righteous road.

Quentin straightened his tie once again and took the left fork of the path. Time to go back to his new home.

What did he still have to do? Not too much, even with the moving truck that would be coming. The faculty housing came furnished with a bed, dresser, desk and so forth. The small den had nothing in it, but Quentin planned to leave that room mostly alone. If he had a place to study and prepare his lecture notes, he'd be fine. The desk would suit his needs.

Dishes, though, he had some of those. A filing cabinet, secondhand but still good enough to use. One battered old recliner. A guilty pleasure, but Quentin did like to sit back and put his feet up for a few minutes after a long day's work. No TV, though. He'd gotten out of the habit of watching during his own years as a student.

And he definitely didn't want to be distracted now that he had so much to focus on in his new position. Oh, dear. Would his roommate be the loud type, prone to playing music at all hours? Would he insist on an entertainment center blaring pictures and sounds? How would he ever get his work done, much less manage to keep up with the classes?

Focus, Quentin, focus. Make this work. Anything is possible if you put your mind to it. You can do this. He ran the mantra of the Center through his mind, reassuring himself.

Thinking with his head down, not really watching where he was going, Quentin ran over syllabi and lists in his mind. Planning for classes beat worrying over an "unorthodox" roommate any day.

He didn't notice anyone in his way until he literally ran into him, bouncing off what felt like a brick wall and reeling back, almost tripping, then steadying himself at the last moment against a tree. "Excuse me," he said automatically, then looked up to see if the person he'd run into needed any help.

Looked up, and felt his traitorous heart skip a beat.

Dear God. If Andy and Ten Hawks were attractive, this man was something from out of a dream. Tall and lean-hipped with broad shoulders, he had the face of an angel and the wicked cast of a devil. Just the sort of man who...who...who could get Quentin into deep, deep trouble.

Although it might be worth the fall...

No. Stop thinking like that. "I'm sorry," Quentin apologized, holding out a hand for the stranger to shake. "I'm Professor Whiteside. Can I help you with something? Are you lost? This is faculty housing, you know. The professors live here." He waved at the tall house they stood in front of.

The stranger's blue eyes twinkled. He tossed a wave of honey-brown hair tipped with magenta streaks out of his face, pulled a pack of cigarettes and a lighter from his pocket, and grinned in a way that made Quentin's treasonous chest thump again. "Nah, I'm fine. You, though, you look like you've seen a ghost. Everything okay?"

"Me? I'm all right." Quentin tried to courteously dodge around the man, who'd lit up and was drawing in with a deeply satisfied air.

Attempting not to breathe the fumes, Quentin looked him up and down, carefully clinical. He might have been handsome—*stop that*—but he couldn't have been more than twenty-one. Probably a student. "Do you need anything?" Quentin repeated himself politely. An idea struck him. "Are you waiting for a professor? I'm the new lecturer in the English department. One of two."

The man chuckled. "Yeah. I'm supposed to take care of moving some things. For another professor." He tipped his cigarette at Quentin. "Call me Lee. I'm supposed to meet Dr. Jennings' truck."

Quentin resisted the urge to roll his eyes. Not only was this Billy late, but he had the nerve to rope a student into moving his things off a truck and into the apartment for him. He must have gotten a key. What if he'd made copies? Oh, oh, that wouldn't be a good thing at all.

Quentin hated to be so tightly wound, but maybe it would be better to keep an eye on Lee. If he had to change the locks...

Lee ambled over to the porch of the small building, once a private home that had been converted in recent years, and hopped up into what looked like a comfortable seat. He kicked his legs idly. "Mind if I wait? I can stay out of your hair." He twined a red-tipped lock around his finger. "Nothing better to do, anyway."

"I'll stay outside with you." Quentin took up position a few feet away, on the other side of the short stairs, and leaned a bit against the edge of the porch. Not too casually, though. He couldn't afford to be seen as informal by the students. That could lead to trouble. The last Father who'd advised him told him not to let students start thinking he was one of them. They'd take advantage.

Quentin wasn't sure, but...

Better not to encourage Lee, anyway. If he were left alone, who knew what he'd do? He seemed content enough to sit and tap ashes off into the grass, but Quentin didn't trust him in a deep, instinctual way. From the tips of his dyed hair to the loose, worn sandals on his feet, he seemed like a wild child and one to watch out for.

A woman, perhaps in her forties, who Quentin recognized as a professor of Economics, came out of the front door and made her way down the stairs. Quentin nodded and smiled at Dr. Framworth. Lee grinned, waved with his cigarette hand and chirped, "What's up, Doc?"

Quentin winced.

Framworth gave Lee a perplexed look and nodded. "Good morning."

"Going for breakfast?"

"I'm afraid I've run out of cream for my coffee." The woman was beginning to smile. Smile!

"God, can't have that. If I don't drink at least half a pot, I'm worthless." Lee took another drag on his smoke. "Bet you can find some at the cafeteria. It's not far."

"I know where it is. I've been teaching here for seven years."

"Aw, what a shame. You don't need an escort, then?"

To Quentin's amazement, Framworth chuckled. "I'll be just fine on my own. Take care, now." She walked away without any questions or even a comment on the smoking. Also, without saying anything else to Quentin.

The slow burn of jealousy started in Quentin's stomach. How could Lee make it so easy to charm people? Quentin tried, himself, he really did, going by the guidelines the Center had drilled in, but...

Lee watched Framworth go, idly scratching at his calf, then puffed thoughtfully for a minute. "So," he asked, idly as if he were wondering about the time, "would you bojangle her?"

"Would I what?" Quentin blinked. It seemed that Lee could salt an innocent question and a slang verb with as much innuendo as three blue jokes. But surely he didn't mean...

"Bojangle. Do. You know, fuck." Lee made an obscene hand gesture with his cigarette. "Would you?"

Quentin felt himself turning pink. "I—I—of course not. I wouldn't think about such a thing. She's my colleague, and it would be most inappropriate."

"Oh, not proper. Too bad." Lee crushed his cigarette out on the edge of the porch, then pulled out his pack again. He tapped it against his palm. "So what about Ten Hawks? I mean, have you seen him? God, he's something else. I'd bojangle him."

"He's the Chancellor," Quentin blurted in horror. His mind instantly flitted to a picture of Ten Hawks with his shirt off, muscled chest gleaming with sweat, and...no. *No, no, no.* "Look here, you really have to stop this. You could get into all sorts of trouble if the wrong person heard you."

"Like you won't report me?" Lee cut Quentin a sly look. "You look pretty law-abiding. Not gonna narc on someone who's out of line?"

"I—I—I—"

"Calm down, take it easy. Don't want you to stroke out on me." Lee lit up another cigarette and drew in until the cherry glowed bright red. "Stress. You need to watch out for stress. It'll kill you faster than these things."

That stung. Quentin tried hard to be calm. "I can take care of myself."

"I think I could really be good with someone to watch over me," Lee sang. He had a surprisingly tuneful voice for someone who smoked as much as he appeared to. "But I don't really think you could call me a lost little lamb."

More like the Big Bad Wolf, Quentin thought, but kept to himself. "If you like." He turned away from Lee, determined not to encourage the boy. Not to look at him. Not to think about what he'd be like when he kissed him, tasting of smoke and probably coffee, soft lips moving under... *No.*

Quentin felt his cock stir. Dear God. Hastily, he untucked his shirt and let it hang loose on the outside of his pants. To make it look a little less stupid, he undid his tie a bit. The day seemed to be heating up. Perhaps he'd change into something roomier and more flexible once his boxes arrived.

Was that a truck? Quentin stood up straighter, peering down the one-lane paved road that curved past the faculty housing. Yes...yes. He heard the sound of a diesel engine. *Finally.*

"That your stuff coming?" Lee asked. "Or maybe it's my cargo. I'm supposed to wait for a delivery van from We-Move-Quick."

"It could be for either of us, then." Quentin had used the popular transport service as well. He looked at his watch. "They're late." He sighed. "Just like my roommate. Unorthodox," he added in a grumble.

"Don't knock the unorthodox. It can be a lot more fun than Average Joe. You look like you try too hard to be Clark Kent. Why not unleash Superman and see how you fly?" Lee hopped down off the porch and vaulted over the stairs. Suddenly he was face-to-face with Quentin, those amazing blue eyes sparkling into Quentin's own. "Bet you can soar." His voice, low and mesmerizing, held Quentin in place.

Lee touched his lips to Quentin's own in a brief, fleeting kiss. Before Quentin had a chance to jerk away on instinct, Lee backed up with a devilish grin. "I think there are two trucks, one for each of us. By the way, I was just kidding earlier. My name's actually William. But hey, you and I are going to be roomies, so you can call me Billy. I think we're going to get along just fine." Billy winked. "Last one to the trucks is an undergraduate!"

And with that he loped away to the approaching vehicles, waving at them and giving a cheerful yell. Quentin stood frozen where Billy had left him, still as a statue, his lips tingling from his fellow professor's light touch of mouth to mouth.

He could feel his heart sinking. *Unorthodox. Blatantly sexual. Oh...God.*

God, what do I do now?

Chapter Two

Quentin's lips still buzzed where Billy had kissed him. They felt as if someone had applied sparkly color and added two or three small spangles. Just like he'd...back in his youth...

He couldn't think about those days now. The Center had taught him how to handle himself. He had to focus on the here and now, and look to the future.

His bedroom had, at least, provided a refuge. Billy had been all too obliging in letting the first set of deliverymen move Quentin's things in first, even if he had plopped down in Quentin's chair and called it "damn good", insisting that it stay in the den.

Quentin hadn't had the strength to protest. Billy's force of personality was too strong to be denied when Quentin was feeling vulnerable. Another flaw of his, drat it. Looking over at the space where he'd intended his comfort spot to be, he felt another twinge of resentment. If the chair stayed outside his room, its soothingly battered cushions and padded arms would get scarred by cigarette burns and start conforming to Billy's behind. Billy's wonderfully tight ass.

"Please stop," Quentin begged himself in a whisper. He rubbed the bridge of his nose to try and ward off a headache. He had a feeling he'd be getting a lot of them, though, with Billy as a roommate. The temptation alone could be the death of him.

He'd have to cling to Melissa. She wasn't much for men who were emotionally needy, but surely she'd understand once he explained everything she needed to know. She did *not* need to know about Billy's good looks, especially from Quentin's perspective. Melissa wasn't crazy about any rivals for her affection, and her disdain for anything remotely homosexual was legendary.

She knew about Quentin's past, and expected him not to falter from the path he'd chosen. A woman who was aware of what he'd been and what he strove to become, she was something he couldn't lose. Not now.

With Melissa as the cornerstone to keep them on track, she and Quentin would have a good life together. Both had neatly outlined their future, following a careful plan. While Melissa completed her law degree, he'd teach for a couple of years and save up some money, as well as publishing enough articles to earn respect and prestige among his peers. They'd put enough aside for a properly attractive house, and once they'd gotten settled they planned to have children. Two, a boy and a girl, if they were lucky. Children they could raise together. Melissa could be hard-nosed, but she would make a wonderful mother.

Quentin had doubts about what kind of father he'd be, but he kept those private. Where Melissa led, he followed. If she wanted the American Dream, he wasn't going to tell her no. She was his salvation, and everything he'd dreamed about when he was being practical.

Seeking comfort, Quentin focused on the picture of his dear girl, poised on the edge of the desk. She'd already been threatened by Quentin's neat stacks of paper, so he pulled the frame a little closer. Touching Melissa's image with one finger, lingering over her precise smile, glossy hair, and compact, trim figure, he smiled.

"I love you," he said—and almost meant the words.

Outside, he heard a crash. The noise made him jump in his seat, knocking one knee against the underside of the desk. Melissa's picture toppled over. Quentin would have set her back upright, but at the moment he wanted to know just what had fallen and how badly something was damaged.

Standing, he walked to the window and peered out. Billy and a deliveryman were laughing over a burst carton that spilled a collection of broken plates onto the lawn. Waving the moving man aside, Billy squatted on the grass and began to pick up pieces of flatware, tossing them back into the box with careless abandon.

So he'd be eating off Quentin's plates, then, wouldn't he?

Quentin bit his lip. He didn't mind sharing. But if Billy broke his as well, he wouldn't be able to afford replacing what was lost, not for a while. He'd spent enough time in college eating off paper towels with plastic spoons and forks. God help him, he didn't want to go back to those days.

Back when he'd...

Melissa. Think about Melissa. In fact... Quentin reached for his cell phone on top of the filing cabinet. Glad that he had managed to get a signal up in the foothills, he hit her number on the speed dial. *Be there. Please, be there.*

Three rings, and a crisp voice answered. "This is Melissa Rife speaking."

"Melissa. Hello. It's Quentin." Going limp with relief, Quentin sank back into his seat. "I hope you don't mind my calling."

"I have a class in fifteen minutes. Can this wait?" Melissa sounded annoyed and impatient. No questions about how his trip up had been, or how he was settling in. But then again, that wasn't her way. Unless someone told her otherwise, she assumed that everything was going according to her plans.

"I just wanted to tell you that I miss you. Are you doing all right?"

"Me? I'm fine, Quentin. Now, did you have anything you needed to talk about?"

Quentin thought fleetingly about Billy, then sighed.

"What was that?"

"What? Oh. Nothing. Don't concern yourself."

"Why did you call me, Quentin?"

"Just to hear the sound of your voice," he replied in all honesty. "As I said, I missed you."

It was Melissa's turn to heave a deep, annoyed breath. "Quentin, I don't have time for this. Of course you miss me. I miss you too. But we've discussed all of this. Everything's in order. Two years, and we'll be together again."

Two years of nothing but phone calls and the occasional visit. But he had to hold on to her. She was his lifeline. "Of course." Quentin hid his disappointment, though he knew he should have expected no less. "I'll let you get back to preparing for class."

"Thank you." Melissa disconnected without a goodbye. Quentin didn't protest. Melissa rarely used unnecessary words. She'd said "I love you" before, not often, but enough for Quentin to believe her. The rest of the time, he took her on faith.

Something else crashed outside. Irritated, Quentin flew to the window to look out. This time the culprit was a box full of old records spilling out in a cascade of faded covers and black discs. Billy still seemed to think this was hilarious. And the way he and the deliveryman bent over the mess to clear it up, their hands brushing against one another...

Quentin swallowed hard. With an effort, he turned away, back to his papers. His first lesson plans. He'd discuss the significance of the historical era in which Jane Austen had begun to write, and then move on to an overview of her works. *Pride and Prejudice, Sense and Sensibility...* Quentin knew the books almost by heart. He had a copy of each, dog-eared and highlighted, read so many times that they were only just held together by the tape down their spines.

He heard the front door slam. From the smell of cigarette smoke wafting in, Billy had arrived. There was a heavy thump as he put something down, and then some tuneful humming. Quentin listened to Billy rummaging through whatever it was he'd carried in. Blessed silence reigned for a moment, and then...*bam, bam, bam.*

It was the final straw. Carefully putting down his lesson plan, not wanting anything to get out of order, Quentin emerged into the den to find Billy cheerfully nailing album covers to the walls, along with other hooks to hang the records themselves on.

"So he's alive," Billy got out around a mouthful of nails. He spat them into his palm and grinned that same cheeky grin, completely at ease. "This is the noisy part. It gets better. So what were you doing, unpacking?"

"Not exactly." Everything Quentin owned had been neatly put away while Billy joked, laughed and smoked with the truck drivers. "I was going over my class notes."

Why he'd volunteered the information, he didn't know. Surely he didn't want to get into a conversation with the man. Billy was dangerous. A temptation that lured him down the path he dared not tread. Living with him would be hard enough. They shouldn't be friends, not if Quentin wanted to stay safe. Pure. Good enough for Melissa.

Billy picked his ever-present cigarette up out of a glass ashtray. He inhaled and exhaled, looking almost blissful. "Hey, hope you don't mind about the smoke. I got hooked on these back in community college. Never have been able to kick the habit, but then again, I don't want to." He winked. "You ever try? They're hell on your lungs, but man, do they relax you. And there's no better place to make friends than around an ashtray between classes. You wouldn't believe how students chill out. You can really get to know them."

"You've taught before?" Quentin was surprised.

"Yeah, did a couple years of quarterlies back at that same tech school. Basic English classes. So many of those kids didn't believe they could write as much as a few paragraphs. I had 'em turning out essays before they were done. Nothing like the look of pride on a student's face when they've done what they thought was impossible. Yeah?"

Quentin had never had the pleasure. The few undergraduate courses he'd lectured in had all been to serious-faced freshmen who, he suspected, had scrambled to keep up. He tried to be hard, like Melissa, but fair. Truth be told, he'd thought they were afraid of him. Just as he was a little afraid of them.

Maybe they really had been cowed into silence. And all the while, irrepressible Billy had been making buddies outside of class.

That slowly smoldering spark of jealousy kindled again.

"Just a few more covers to nail up. I figured you could have the opposite wall for whatever you want to hang. Maybe an art print? You look like that kind of guy. Hey, am I going to get lucky with some Rubenesque ladies? All that pretty pink skin with the naughty bits all plump and perky?"

Quentin felt his cheeks grow warm. "I don't... I mean, I haven't..." He didn't own anything to put on the walls. Art was a potential snare for the unwary. His only decoration, a large dry-erase board, had already been hung in his bedroom.

"Nope? Eh, no worries. You'll find something you like." Billy winked and went back to hammering, whistling something that Quentin vaguely recognized from his younger days as Pink Floyd. He hovered for a minute, watching...staring at the play of muscles in Billy's arms...the way he moved, so confident and sure of himself...his strong legs, braced so that he could do his work...

Oh, God, I've got to get out of here.

"Excuse me. I need some fresh air," Quentin fumbled. "I'll just go and—"

"Yeah. It is getting kinda foggy, huh? I'll open a window after I'm done. This place is gonna feel just like home, Superman."

"Please don't call me that."

"Okay, Clark."

"That either." Quentin felt his thin layer of composure evaporating. He headed for the door. "Don't mind me, I'll just...I'll be outside."

"Your call, man." Billy hammered on, putting the nails back into his mouth. He lipped them just the way he would a cigarette, his mobile lips cradling the iron as if he were sucking on a...his mouth full of...

Quentin fled for the great outdoors.

He had enough sense to stop on the porch, although he did put a hand to his head to steady himself. Fastidious, not wanting to disarrange his clothing, he sat on the edge of the porch. Folding his hands between his knees, he took in a deep breath of clean air and waited for his head to clear.

Footsteps were his first clue that someone was approaching. "Quentin, hey!" a familiar drawl exclaimed. Andy. "They actually had some semi-fresh strawberries in the caf this morning, and some decent company. The professors are always relaxed right before a new semester. I stayed for a few cups of coffee." Andy kept talking until he was standing next to Quentin. The man touched him on one shoulder. "Hey, you okay? You look kind of pale."

Quentin struggled for equilibrium. "I'm fine," he said with one of his carefully practiced smiles. "Billy's a bit of a chain-smoker, and I'm not used to the fumes. I needed a minute to clear my head, that's all."

"Billy, yeah." Andy stuck his hands in his pockets and looked at the housing. He tilted his head to the side and listened to the sounds of a hammer banging nails into a wall. "I warned you, but I guess words don't measure up to the reality. Think you two can get along without killing each other?"

"That remains to be seen." Quentin froze. One could not reveal too much about oneself, not until they were sure of the other conversationalist's goals. "I mean, I'm sure we'll be just fine after some adjustment."

"Quentin, man. Move over." Andy nudged him. "There's room up here for two. Come on, let me have a seat."

Quentin moved as he was directed, although the steps weren't *that* big and when Andy sat down, they were hip-to-hip and shoulder-to-shoulder.

Andy sniffed at Quentin's shirt. Sniffed! Far too up close and personal. "Whoo, yeah. Billy must be hell with the smokes. That all that's bothering you? 'Cause you might be able to play the brave little soldier, but you don't fool me. What's on your mind?"

Quentin flashed on images of Billy and the way he'd looked both playing around and working hard alongside the movers. The kind of man he'd...have had a crush on, back in the bad old days. Weak, weak, weak. The pill tasted bitter going down.

But he wasn't like that anymore. He wasn't.

"Honestly, I'm fine." He nodded to emphasize his point. "Don't worry about me." *Please, don't ask any awkward questions.*

"If you say so, friend." Andy sat for a minute in companionable silence before speaking again. "Billy's pretty wild, although I'm guessing you figured that out already. If he weren't a complete and total genius, even Ten Hawks might have thought twice about hiring him."

"He does seem a little out of the ordinary," Quentin ventured cautiously.

Andy hooted. "That's putting it mildly. Billy's a rebel with a clue, a cause and a mission. But the students love him. You know he's won three or four teaching awards? He'll probably put them on your mantelpiece."

Quentin thought back to his one printed nomination for an award. The jealousy uncurled, beginning to burn his insides. "Really."

"Yeah." Andy kicked the step with the toe of his sneaker. "Don't worry. You'll win a dozen of your own. Ten Hawks couldn't stop talking about his two fantastic additions to the department."

Quentin brightened a little at the bit of news, but remained cautious. It wouldn't do to look too eager to curry favor. "You know him well?"

"Can't help but know Ten Hawks. He gets involved with everyone. I think he likes me more than the others, though. See, I help him with the books from time to time, when neither he nor his secretary can figure things out. The man's an administrative genius, but not so good with the numbers. Don't tell him I told you that, though."

Quentin felt stung. He'd learned his lessons about secrecy and privacy. Gossip, too, come to that. Failing again. "I'd never say such a thing."

"Didn't figure you would. But hey, about Billy. From what I hear, the thing is just to take him as he is, and then you'll get along just fine." Andy stood, stretching. "I've got to get to my office on the main campus. No rest for the wicked, right? All the professors are together in one building, so we shouldn't be far from each other. Just knock on my door if you want to have lunch or something."

Quentin rarely ate lunch. He never had time to. The habit had peeled away pounds he couldn't afford to lose, leaving him slimmer than he'd have liked, especially considering his slight stature. He tugged at one short lock of hair and fiddled with his collar, stalling for time. "If I'm there, I'll come and get you," he said, the best he could do without the chance to prepare an otherwise adequate answer.

"Good deal. Okay, see you then. I'm blowing this popsicle stand." Andy walked down the steps onto the path and headed away. Quentin watched him go with an unsettled feeling. Ten Hawks and Andy were close. Andy had sat so snugly against Quentin. The feel of another man pressed against him had...

No.

"Hey, Q-man," Billy shouted from inside. "You mind lending a hand? This recliner of yours is damn heavy."

His chair. Quentin scrambled up from the steps and hurried back in the front door. The door to his and Billy's apartment stood ajar, smoke curling through it. As he pushed that door open, he saw Billy sprawled indolently in Quentin's beloved chair. The ashtray sat on his lap and he was crushing out a cigarette. "The second set of moving guys will be coming in with my stuff any minute. I figure we need to push this thing over so there'll be room for my couch."

"I could take the recliner into my room," Quentin offered hopefully.

"Nah. I can tell you've loved this thing hard." Billy patted one of the worn arms. "Gotta have a good place to sit while you're unwinding, right? I like to spread my papers out on the floor. That couch is great for it. Lots of room. So we need to get you an open space."

"I'd planned on doing my work in my bedroom."

Billy raised an eyebrow. "You're shitting me. Those desks are too little for anything like what we'll need. I don't know about you, but the classes I'll be teaching are required for undergraduates. That's a hell of a lot of midterms. Nah. You need to be in here, where there's room." He grinned charmingly. "I won't even smoke while you're grading. Deal?"

Quentin was at a loss for words. He felt himself curl up inside, trying to hide from the blunt force of Billy's personality.

But there was also indignation. Who did Billy think he was to run roughshod over Quentin's preferences?

He would have spoken up, words drawn from his lessons, but Billy had already moved on. "And what about company?" Billy waggled his tongue. "You need room to woo a hot honey." He licked his lips. Quentin had a brief flash in which he wondered what it would be like to feel that tongue probing inside his mouth, twining around his own.

Don't. Quentin shook his head to clear it. "That won't be necessary. I have a girlfriend. Nearly a fiancée. We're almost engaged. I'll be saving what I can to buy her a ring."

"Taken, huh? That's a shame. Lots of gorgeous guys and girls down in the town. This is a pretty artsy place, fancy-free, and from what I've heard the whole bunch just love to have a good time." Billy tossed his hair, the magenta streaks flying in a dazzling pattern before they settled back into place. "But nah, you don't look like someone who'd go bar-hopping." He winked. "We'll have to work on that."

"I'd rather we didn't," Quentin said firmly, regaining the inner strength he'd been taught. "Please. I came up here for a quiet, ordinary teaching position. I'm not interested in making friends or winning over my students. I just want to be left alone so I can do my job."

"So you're saying you don't need anyone to keep you warm at night?"

"I can call my—Melissa—anytime I want to."

"Long-distance relationships leave a cold bed, man."

"It's good enough for us. Why can't you just leave it alone?" Quentin rubbed his temple. "Why do you have to be so... Please, Dr. Jennings."

"Billy."

"Dr. Jennings," Quentin insisted. "We're roommates, nothing more. I'll ask you to respect that. I don't want to be your friend, or your confidante, or anything else. We share a space because that's the assignment the college made. Other than that, let's just try to stay out of each other's way. Agreed?"

"Damn, there go all my plans to get you drunk and naked." Billy stood up casually and stretched like a lazy lion. "You want to keep this on a business level, fine. But hey, don't go cramping my style. I'll live by your rules if you'll let me be myself."

Quentin wanted to protest, but didn't see how he could. Fair was fair, after all. "Very well," he said after a moment's pause. As much as he'd have preferred a quiet, nonsmoking roommate, he had to deal with the cards he'd been given. If Billy left him alone, he'd be all right.

He had to be.

"Life will place many obstacles in your path," Quentin remembered Father Andrew saying as he tugged on his beard. *"Your challenge is to avoid them or push them out of harm's reach. Then, you'll be able to function as a normal, cleanly motivated individual. You'll see."*

Quentin took comfort in and clung to the words.

Outside, a second truck pulled up in the drive. Billy glanced out the window and grinned broadly. "My turn for the big stuff. You might want to hang out in the kitchen, Quentin. Gotta let the deliveryman do his work."

"Of course." Being polite was permitted—nay, encouraged—to demonstrate how one was overcoming their challenges. "I'll just have a snack."

Billy hooted. "Got the munchies? That's cool. By the way, I had to move some of your food and shit so I could fit my own supplies in. Hope you don't mind." Without waiting for an answer, he bounded for the door and pulled it open. "Hey, big mover-type guy! Bring that in this way, my man."

Quentin beat a hasty retreat into the kitchen. Once there, he leaned on the folding table they would eat from, and took a few deep, calming breaths. He concentrated hard until the sound of Billy's chattering and the movers' responses faded into a background hum.

Closing his eyes, he relaxed a little. The temptation to think about Billy faded once he was away from the man. This wasn't a hopeless situation, then, was it? He could do anything he set his mind to, couldn't he?

And he was hungry. Opening a cabinet, the one where he'd left his cereal, he reached for the box of Grape-Nuts—and stopped. There were a bunch of bananas and a liter of pop sitting in the way. A box of microwave popcorn and a bag of nacho chips. One lonely can of peas. His personal supply of food had been pushed all the way to the back.

Billy!

His temper fraying around the edges, Quentin stormed back out of the kitchen. "Billy, this won't work. You said you moved a few things around. And you don't put fruit in a cupboard, for heaven's sake. What on earth were you thinking of?" He stopped in his tracks. "Oh."

Billy and the moving man, a strong-bodied Mexican with long hair and a roughly handsome face, were wrapped around each other. Arms and legs had been tangled together. Billy's hand was twined in the mover's hair as he held the man close to kiss him.

Quentin felt his mouth go dry and his unreliable cock begin to fill. *Oh...God.* The sight of the two standing there, completely oblivious to everything around them, made him feel too warm and somehow exposed. They were so at ease with themselves and not minding a bit about anyone else seeing what they were doing.

Billy broke the kiss off first, trailing his hand down to rub the mover's back. "Great service," he cracked. "And you even do it with a smile."

The man replied in Spanish. Billy rattled off a long string of syllables without blinking.

Then, as if he'd known Quentin was watching, Billy turned with a saucy swing of his hips and waved. "This is Enrique. He's going to help me get things arranged. Don't mind us. At least I'm being quiet, right?" He sparkled with good-natured mischief. "Oh, by the way, you might have noticed. I'm gay. Pink sparkles and tutu and mixed drinks and everything. But hey, it won't be a problem, right?"

Quentin found himself completely without anything to say. The Center had warned him to stay away from temptation, but with Billy he'd be faced by it nearly twenty-four seven. And watching the two men, his cock almost sat up and begged for the show to go on.

Father Andrew, guide me. He was in deep, deep trouble, wasn't he?

Chapter Three

"Mmm." Billy's laugh was like a lion's purr—low, rumbling—but at the same time sexually appealing as a siren's call. "You ready for this?"

"After watching you all day? *Si*, I'm ready." Enrique had a deeper voice, almost a baritone. He'd been singing earlier, some soft tune in Spanish, barely audible during the clatter of clunks and clanks coming from two men moving around in a space designed for one.

Both men seemed to be in the best of moods, something Quentin could not claim for himself. He'd shut the door to his bedroom and opened the window, hoping the combination would block out some of the noise, but no luck. His room and Billy's were side by side, and it appeared that the walls were thin. Very, very thin.

What fun. He'd be treated to a live show. His brain argued against the idea, but his cock approved. It rose up full and thick inside his pants, creating a tent against the zipper. Just like a dog that wanted to play. Quentin resisted the urge to thump himself, as he knew how badly that would hurt, and tried to remain calm.

He wasn't a prude. God knew he'd overheard people having sex before. A certain episode in his undergraduate years came to mind, when he'd woken after a restless dream to hear his roommate busily fucking away on the top bunk, while he lay in the lower one. Neither the boy nor his girlfriend had been the least bit shy about making noise.

Back then, it had been acutely embarrassing. Now, it was disturbingly exciting. Perhaps because it had been so long since he'd partaken of any pleasure with Melissa.

Quentin sighed. He ran his hand over his face, rubbing at the bridge of his nose, and tried to get on with his evening just as if the other room were quiet. Undressing for bed came first. He'd made the narrow mattress up with his best set of clean sheets and blanket, and a plumped pillow beckoned invitingly. Sliding between those comforting coverings would be heaven.

Slowly, Quentin unzipped his trousers. He had some difficulty easing the fastening down over his erection, but then again, he'd had plenty of practice in the past. Long past, thank God. He managed the feat without flinching, even though Billy and Enrique chose that moment to begin loudly kissing, murmuring endearments in both English and Spanish.

"Diablo, you are…"

"Just like that. You know the way."

"You taste like the cigarette, but you are sweet, yes?"

"Try me again and see what you think."

Quentin kept trying to ignore the pair as he toed off his shoes, slid the pants from his legs, then removed his socks. Everything that was dirty went neatly into a hamper with only one burst side, arranged so that the hole faced a wall. The loose, thin sweatshirt he'd changed into for moving things needed a wash, so after he pulled it over his head and had it off, that went into the hamper too.

Standing there nearly naked, Quentin felt as exposed as if he'd just walked into a classroom undressed. Billy and Enrique's running commentary, along with sounds that brought

37

back vivid pictures and memories, didn't help. It was like living in a whorehouse and listening to someone else ply their trade.

The mere fact that Billy had chosen to spend the night with this moving man boggled Quentin's mind. As far as he knew, the two had only met earlier that day. What kind of people were they to go and have sex in such an appalling hurry? They couldn't have met more than a day or so previous when Enrique first loaded his truck. True, Enrique was a handsome man, and Quentin couldn't imagine anyone saying no to Billy, but still...

Quentin looked down at his cock, insistently pressing against the front of his boxers, and sighed. Normally he'd skin out of the shorts too and put on a pair of pajamas, preferably something Melissa had bought him or guided his choice on. Somehow, though, he didn't want to stand there vulnerably while he took the time to open a drawer, so with a slight wince of distaste he went to the bed with his boxers on and slipped beneath the covers.

For a moment, the pleasure of being between cool, pale blue sheets and light gray blanket, with the puffy pillow cradling his head, took Quentin away. Away from a sticky Indian summer at Sweetwater and off to a safe place, where he didn't have to think about the bad old days or face their present-day reminders. He exhaled a long breath and got comfortable, finding the mattress to be much softer than it looked. It could cradle a man and give him some peace of mind before he slept.

He was just about to relax completely when the noise started again next door. "Take those clothes off," Billy ordered. "I want to see you naked. Every inch of all those muscles."

"Only if you strip as well. Fair is fair, eh?"

"Who says we have to play by the rules? I want to sit here and take in the sights. All that delicious skin revealed one inch at a time."

Quentin heard Enrique's bass laugh. "All right. So you want a show. Fine, then, a show you get. But then I want you to be naked too."

"Believe me, I plan on it."

Quentin could almost see Billy's face, sparkling with mischief, as he leaned back in his personal comfy chair—which had *not* been appropriated for the den. Perhaps he'd be spreading his legs wide, resting his hand over the bulge in his jeans...

Quentin closed his eyes tightly. Instead of listening, he deliberately tried to distract himself. Melissa. He had to think of Melissa.

Melissa—the beautiful, the bold, the brave. He knew that people who didn't like his girlfriend called her a bitch, but he'd stood up to defend her honor more than once. Melissa was just a strong woman who had no problem voicing her opinions, and he'd been glad to defend her for it.

Granted, she'd usually raked him down for his pains, claiming she could take care of herself. Quentin accepted that about her too. Melissa didn't need anyone. The fact that she'd taken Quentin on as part of her life was something he remained grateful for.

She was his guide, now; she was part of his salvation.

Trying to block out the sounds from the room next door, slithery noises of clothes being shed one piece at a time along with Billy's raucous version of "The Stripper", Quentin turned his mind to the time that he and Melissa had first met.

It was over a lunch table in the cafeteria, during his last year of graduate school. She was younger than him, still working on pre-law, but old enough to know her own mind. She'd seated herself at his table without asking, looked him over as if weighing him in the balance as a worthy companion, and then struck up a conversation leading in a decisive direction. "You're in the Ph.D. program, correct? What do you plan on doing with your life? Do you feel like going to dinner tonight to discuss this?"

Such boldness had stolen his breath. From there, everything had unfolded so naturally. She'd wanted to go to dinner and a movie, and Quentin had been so startled and flattered that he'd scraped up the money to treat her. She was a beautiful woman bound to a mission.

He knew, granted, that he was only a part of Melissa's long list of life goals. Find a man who'd be a success and an asset in a marriage—a distinguished professor—check. His past was a stumbling block, but Melissa had judged him to be rehabilitated enough to work with. And she did care for him, he was sure of it, especially when he clung to her during the times that things grew hard to handle.

The few times they'd had sex had been...well, not earth-shattering, but certainly satisfying—if accompanied by an illicit guilt. Father Andrew would not have approved of sexual liaisons outside the bonds of matrimony, even if the parties involved were male and female.

Every time, Quentin had been careful about making sure Melissa was fully satiated before seeing to his own pleasure. Ah, the sense memory of how her hands felt scratching down his back—wonderful. She had sharp nails that left raised welts in their wake, but Quentin wore the marks like badges of honor.

Despite Father Andrew's inner reprimands against sins of the flesh, the marks from making love to Melissa meant something. Scratches from a woman's hand were concrete badges of honor he wore to prove he wasn't what he had once been. Proof that he could start fresh and leave his past behind.

"There, I have undressed. Do you like what you see?" Enrique sounded teasing. An image of the man, naked, flashed into Quentin's mind. He'd have strong limbs corded with muscle, the day's sweat dried on his skin. His smell would be strong and salty—Quentin almost imagined he got a whiff of the aroma of pure male.

He turned his head into the pillow and inhaled the scent of soapy laundry detergent instead.

His nose might be placated, but his mind kept bringing up images. He could all but see Enrique turning around in a slow circle, arms at his sides, slightly raised so Billy could see everything. His cock would be long and thick, probably uncut, and already hard. How long? More than seven inches. Through that coverall, at least a size too small, Quentin had seen...

No. Think about Melissa.

There wasn't an inch of Melissa's body that Quentin hadn't paid extremely close attention to. He knew her all the way from her petite but proud breasts to the neatly trimmed patch of dark curls between her thighs, what lay beneath the tuft of hair, and her defined legs, kept hard and slim through daily jogs.

And her face...well, again, she could be hard, but nothing disguised her beauty. A practical oval shape with a straight nose and a small but kissable mouth, plus big brown eyes that never betrayed what she was thinking. He loved her mystery, something she never dropped even when they were having sex or when he simply wanted to kiss her.

She appreciated the gesture when he went down on her, Quentin was sure of it. He'd learned to like the salty taste of a woman, and been careful in his study of what pleased her and what didn't. He had it down to an art now, knowing exactly where to lick and where to flick, where to suck and where to use his fingers.

Melissa didn't like the word pussy, though. Too crude for her. She either didn't refer to her genitalia at all, choosing to direct Quentin by pushes on his shoulders to move him down, or in less heated moments using the more clinical term of vagina.

He hadn't minded. Anything to stay in her good graces.

Clinging to her strict direction kept him from going back to what he'd been.

"Ah, so now it is your turn," Enrique teased. Quentin imagined that he could hear a slick sound, as if Enrique were stroking his cock with a handful of lotion or some such. "I want to see you as you have seen me."

"Fair enough." There came the squeak of chair springs from Billy standing up. "You stand there and keep on doing what you're doing."

"Don't want to come too fast, friend."

"You won't. Besides, even if you do, I bet a man like you can go all night."

Enrique laughed. "You bet I can. Especially when I've got a tasty treat like you to lick up and down."

"Ooh, there's going to be licking. I'd better get these clothes off in a hurry, hadn't I?"

"Tease."

"Damn right I am. But I never leave a man in trouble for long," Billy boasted.

Quentin heard the rustling sound of clothes being shucked off, then some soft noises of a shirt and pants hitting the wall next to his bed.

Billy spoke again. "See? I'm ready, willing and able."

"Oh, yes, you are. Let me touch you. That fat cock of yours is *bueno. Le deseo.*"

"You're going to have me. I'll shove my dick so far up inside of you that you'll taste me in the back of your throat."

"Oh, so you think you're going to be the one on top? We may have an argument here, *amigo.*"

"I'm always on top." Billy sounded cocky and brazen as ever. "Don't tell me you've never bottomed."

"Not often. Although for you, I could be tempted."

"How about if I suck this big long prick first? Would that get you in a good mood for the fuck of your life?"

"Promises, promises. Do you swear you will deliver?"

"Do you? I want that payload in my mouth. Heavy, thick come pouring over my tongue."

"Ah, you push me beyond what I can be expected to bear."

There were two soft thumps, as if Billy had gone down on his knees. "Hang on," he said huskily. "Here comes the ride of your life."

Sucking, licking noises started, along with a series of deep groans from Enrique. Quentin fisted his hands in his covers and tried not to listen.

God help him if he could stop himself, though. It brought back memories of nights when he had...with another man, smelling so rich and heavy...sparkle on his cheekbones, liner around his eyes, and his hair a shade of green not found in nature.

Quentin's cock gave a twitch, the way it always did when he let himself slip and think about those days when he'd been so wild and so incautious. With a wrench, he stopped himself from thinking about those times and focused instead on the people who'd helped him straighten himself out when he'd gone to them for help.

The Center.

Quentin knew that activists generally ran such establishments down as deplorably dehumanizing, but for Quentin, they'd been exactly what he'd been in need of. Plenty of people were comfortable being gay, but he didn't—couldn't—fit into that mold.

The deprogrammers had been the ones to encourage him to stop wearing sparkling makeup and to wash his face clean. Helped him dye his hair back to its natural brown until the green grew out. Spent nights with him, holding his hand, after he'd been invited to one party or another.

He'd obeyed their advice, and never thought about being with another man again.

That was, until he arrived at Sweetwater College. Now, it seemed that everything was coming flooding back as sure as Enrique would pour his essence down Billy's eager throat.

Quentin lay quiet and still as he could while the sucking noises went on and Enrique started to babble in Spanish. He counted the ticking of the second hand on his watch, lying on the bedside table, and passed away the minutes while focusing on that sound. It went on...and on...and on...

God, but Enrique had stamina. When Quentin let his focus slip, he could still hear Billy's mouth messily devouring the Mexican's cock, hungry noises that burned a track into his brain. He couldn't help envisioning that prick sliding in and out between Billy's mobile lips, Billy's cheeks hollowing and bulging as he sucked on the downstroke and let his mouth fill on his way back up.

Quentin's dick throbbed uncomfortably. He ground his teeth.

"*Dios mio!*" Enrique shouted. There was a clatter, as if he'd grabbed at something that went flying. He rattled off a long string of Spanish syllables that ended in a deep, almost painful-sounding groan, and trailed off into Billy's soft laughter.

"Told you." Billy sounded obnoxiously smug. "I'm the undisputed champion of sucking cock."

"Ay...you are good at what you do. Now I have to wonder what happens next. You going to put that baseball bat between your legs to good use?"

"I knew I'd have you begging for it. Lie down on the bed, Enrique. On your back. I want to watch your face while I fuck you."

Footsteps crossed the floor. Billy's bed creaked under the weight of a solid man, then groaned in protest as Billy added his own weight. "Lube and condoms are in the drawer to your side. Get one for me, then put it on my cock. You slick me up and I'll slick you down." He paused. "You need much stretching? I bet you do, since you're always on the top."

More Spanish. Quentin recognized a few curse words in the stream of sound. "Shut up and fuck me."

"My pleasure."

A bottle of something clicked open, and then slippery noises started. Enrique cried out in something between pleasure and pain, followed by Billy's murmured reassurances. Quentin could see it so clearly—Billy's fingers moving in and out of that tight, rounded ass, scissoring wide to open the way for his cock to plunge—

Oh, God.

Quentin realized that he'd wrapped his fist around his own cock and had started to pump it nice and slow, timing his pulls to the sounds from next door. He stopped, heat flooding his cheeks. What kind of pervert was he? Look how far he'd fallen.

45

No one decent should get off on listening to two men fuck one another.

He tried to be angry at them, but found that he couldn't. His traitorous cock was pounding with blood, demanding to be satisfied. Father Andrew had frowned on masturbation, but God, Quentin had never been able to stop. Maybe if he concentrated on his own dick and worked on bringing himself to a satisfactory conclusion, he'd be able to ignore the fucking going on next door.

"Ai!" Enrique's howl split the air.

Right, that was it. Quentin threw off the covers and wriggled his hips until he was free of the boxers. He didn't have any lotion or a similar substitute handy to make his hand slick enough to make this really enjoyable, but he'd do his best.

He lay back, closed his eyes and thought of Melissa. She liked riding him, rather than being underneath. If he concentrated hard enough, he could almost see her sitting astride him, and pretend that his own firm grip was the tight, clenching warmth of her womanhood. Oh, yes, Melissa.

No more of his misunderstood young-adult sexuality issues. He had a woman, or rather she had him, and he was on the right track.

Jerking himself off with quick, steady movements, Quentin kept up his fantasy and thought he was doing pretty well, even as his climax began to creep up on him. Melissa, with her dark hair loose and swinging. Small drops of sweat on her creamy white skin. His own hands guiding her hips as she rose and fell on the length of his dick. The way her fingers would pinch and rub at her nipples, something she wouldn't let him do—but he understood her quirks, and tried not to mind.

Yet, no matter how hard he pumped himself, he couldn't seem to produce an orgasm. He knew there was one in wait, coiled and ready at the base of his spine, but it wouldn't rocket up into his balls and out the length of his shaft.

Frustrated, he stopped for a moment. The second he did, the sounds of Billy fucking Enrique rushed in on him, loud as a concert, bringing up almost crystal-clear images. Billy would be on his knees, pushing Enrique's thighs wide apart. His cock would be plunging in and out of a tight brown hole, the opening greedily swallowing his length. Both men would be glistening with sweat, great huge drops that ran down their backs and chests.

This was wrong, so wrong, but impossible to resist. Quentin slowly began to work his erection again. His cock tingled, just as his lips had earlier when Billy kissed him. He closed his eyes, unable to deny himself the pure pleasure, even though he knew it was wrong, wrong, wrong. God help him!

Heavy breathing drowned out the sound of his watch's soothing tick. "Going to come," Billy said roughly. "You want this load up your ass?"

"Want, fuck, yes, want."

"Get ready for me. Open wide, wider. Good. God, yes. So good."

"Come for me, *amor.* You are so beautiful. You almost make me hard again..."

"Good. This night isn't over yet," Billy promised.

Quentin couldn't help but picture Billy tossing his remarkable streaked hair out of his eyes as his hips snapped forward, slick sounds filling the air.

"Coming, Enrique," Billy warned. "Coming now. Oh, God, oh, God, oh God..."

There was a pause, and then both men groaned loudly. Billy let out a whooping war cry, and then all was silent except for the sound of their breathing.

Quentin couldn't take it anymore. He pulled hard on his cock and felt himself explode into orgasm, more come than he'd thought possible pouring from his cock, wetting not only his hand but his belly, thick stripes decorating his torso. His head buzzed with sound and his vision faded into a vista of fizzy darkness.

When he came to himself, he was panting. Deep, ragged breaths. His fist felt as if it had conformed to the shape of his cock, and his fingers ached when he slowly released them. Unable to move any more just yet, he lay still and struggled to catch his breath.

Then, he heard a pounding on the wall. "Hey, didn't realize these walls were so thin, you voyeur, you." Billy chortled. "Want to come and join us?" he asked, the very devil adding a note of temptation and teasing to his voice. "Sounded like you were having a good time listening in, and there's enough of us to go around."

Heat flooded Quentin's cheeks and he groaned as quietly as he could.

Facing Billy the next morning and pretending nothing had happened would have been hard enough. Now, though, he thought it would be impossible. Billy had *heard* him. Oh, God, had he said something when he came? *Please, no.* He couldn't have borne it if he'd said something aloud to betray himself.

Ignoring Billy's teasing question, Quentin grabbed a handful of tissues and roughly scrubbed himself clean of the spunk that had decorated his body. Tossing them into the trash can beside his bed, he rolled over and tugged the covers snugly up around himself.

"Ah, don't tease. Doesn't sound like he wants to play. He's probably half asleep, man," Enrique chided.

"Maybe so. Sounded like a good one. You want to go again? Looks like it to me. But we keep it quiet, okay?"

"You gonna let me fuck you this time?"

"It's against my rules, but hell, you never do know, do you? The night's still young and anything is possible."

Quentin tried his hardest to concentrate on sleep. On Melissa. On anything except what was happening next door.

Because, God help him, he'd *liked* it. And he'd been trying so hard to be the man he expected himself to be.

But it looked like he was starting to backslide, and no, no, no, he couldn't, he wouldn't, he *wouldn't...*

Chapter Four

"It's seven fifty-three on this bright August morning. Welcome to the Morning Show with Ed, Ed and Julie. If you're late for work, better hurry. But hey, if you don't have anything better to do, stick around. We've got the top ten hits on the way, and—"

Quentin opened one eye. The other side of his face was buried in his extremely comfortable pillow.

However, he could clearly see the clock.

Seven fifty-three, as the radio announcer had said. Right on the money, and almost two hours later than he'd planned to get up.

"Damn," he swore under his breath, the curses unfamiliar on his tongue after so long but coming far too easily. "Damn, damn, damn." Tension gripped him hard in its fist and rattled his bones. "Billy."

Whose fault had it been that he'd lain awake almost all night long?

Who'd gone back for a second and third round of wall-shaking sex with fits of laughter, incessant chattering and chain-smoking in between, despite their promises to keep the lid on?

Who had deprived him of so much rest that he'd slept through his alarm?

Billy.

Quentin threw off his blanket and sheet with a growl. He wasn't a violent man by nature, and didn't enjoy confrontation, but if Billy had been standing next to his bed just then, he'd have gotten a kick in the groin and a fist to the nose. Late on his very first day. Late! Quentin was never late. He made a point of punctuality, especially after Melissa had impressed upon him how important it was to always be on time.

He kicked the remainders of his covers free and stood. Taking a deep breath, he ran his hands through the short brown prickles of his hair to calm himself. Violence never solved anything. The horrid situation he'd gotten into, the one that sent him running from the deplorable "gay" scene toward the light...

There had been a man who'd been trouble—Quentin knew—but he'd been unable to help himself. A man who'd known his personal sexual desires were wrong, but hadn't been able to deny them.

Quentin hadn't understood. So oblivious! He'd gone about things misguidedly, not listening to the man's doubts, encouraging him instead to "just relax".

Bad advice.

In the end, the man who'd preyed on Quentin had tried to shoot him. In a flurry of passion, he had then turned the gun on himself. His shot at Quentin only went through the shoulder. The bullet used on himself drove deeply into his brain, ending his life in a heartbeat.

Despite his terror and shock, the realization had been immediate and stark. Quentin knew, beyond any shadow of doubt, that he had driven a confused man to death.

In the aftermath, Quentin's mild wounds had been doctored at a hospital, but it was while he recovered—still in shock over what had happened—that a visitor from the Sainted Lady, who had heard about his plight, came to show him the error of his ways and saved his soul...

But that was history. A hard lesson learned. Now, Quentin had to deal with the present. If he and Billy were to get along at all, he'd have to sit down with the man and have a civilized, hopefully quiet talk about some house rules.

Yes. He'd just get dressed and make himself some breakfast. A healthy mind required a healthy body, and skipping the morning meal, the most important of the day, simply wouldn't do. He'd eat his cereal with perhaps a banana and think about how to broach the subject that night. That wouldn't do anything about his lateness, but at least he'd be prepared to face the day.

That was...unless Billy got in his way.

But surely Billy wouldn't be up and about already. Unorthodox probably extended to sleeping in far past eight and keeping a haphazard set of office hours. Speaking of which, honestly, shouldn't Ten Hawks have been a little more direct in his warning? Living with Billy was like being back in a student dormitory, not sharing an apartment with a fully ranked professor.

Quentin ran a hand down his stomach and grimaced when he hit a crusted spot. Dried-on semen. And he'd thought he'd cleaned himself up the night before. Fine, then, he'd take the time for a shower. A quick one, but thorough.

Grabbing up a towel, one of the good sort which Melissa had bought him and warned him not to leave displayed where others could steal them, Quentin opened the door and set foot out in the small hallway, headed for the bathroom. The door was slightly ajar and the lights off. He pushed it open, expecting an empty room.

He was wrong.

"Holy shit, man!" Billy exclaimed, then laughed. Quentin caught a glimpse of the man tucking himself back into his pair of jockey briefs. "You wanna knock or something when you head in here? Not that I mind you getting a look at the goods, but a guy likes a little privacy when he's taking a whiz."

Quentin began to simmer. "You were relieving yourself with the door open and the lights off?"

"Well, hey, I just woke up, you know? Enrique's still asleep. Lights are too damn bright before I get my first cup of coffee." Billy busied himself with washing his hands at the sink. "Nice body there, Professor. You work out?"

The urge to cover himself with his arms almost overcame Quentin. He managed to stand there stiffly, deliberately not looking at the way the tight black cotton hugged Billy's ass while he waited for the man to finish. "I lift weights. When the weather permits, I jog." Melissa had taught him to love running. When they'd last gone out together, he'd finally been able to keep up with her. The woman could sprint like an ocelot.

"Very cool." Billy shook off his hands, splattering water, and reached for a small towel hanging on a hook. After he'd dried his fingers, he re-hung the terrycloth at a crooked angle.

Quentin itched to straighten it out.

"We should run together some day," Billy offered blithely. "If you ever want to. And hey, remember knocking next time. I'm gonna get a cup of java and fry up something for breakfast." He wiggled his eyebrows. "Sorry about the noise, but Enrique and I worked up a pretty good appetite, if you know what I mean."

"I know. I heard you. All night long."

Billy burst into chuckles. "Nothing like a man with endurance, huh? Or, in your case, a woman. Gotta love it when they can go for hours." He pounded Quentin on the shoulder, just as if they were friends. The warmth of his hand seemed to leave a print on Quentin's skin. "Bathroom's all yours, friend."

I am not your friend.

"Thank you," Quentin said despite his rising anger. "I'll be sure to shut the door."

"Oh, yeah, yeah, sure. Not like I'm going to sneak in here and ogle you naked, right?" Billy winked and sauntered off, his perfectly rounded ass outlined in clear relief through the jockey shorts. "Enrique, you feel like some bacon?" he called.

Quentin shut the bathroom door. And locked it. God, not only was Billy a night owl, but a morning person as well. Insult to injury.

Why did he have a feeling that the day could only go downhill from there?

CR03SO

Clean from head to toe and dressed in his version of office casual—a crisp white button-down shirt over a Sweetwater T-shirt, paired with fresh new khakis—Quentin emerged from his room and aimed himself toward the kitchen. He could hear the sounds of pans clattering and smell the aroma of oily, greasy food thick in the air.

He wouldn't let it get to him. He'd have his cereal and be on his way.

"Enrique, you're sure you have to go so soon?" Billy was asking as Quentin rounded the corner. He got an eyeful of the professor hanging on to the moving man, swinging by his waist. "Bet the moving company would understand if you took another day."

"The boss is already gonna be plenty pissed that I stayed overnight. You are *el Diablo,* so tempting." As Quentin watched, Enrique planted a kiss on Billy's forehead. "I have to get back to work. Wild night, though, eh? I ever come back into town, we should do this again."

"Count on it." Billy was all but purring. He slid his hands up Enrique's back and tilted his head to give the man a thorough kiss. The moving man gave in without a struggle, pulling Billy close. Quentin saw their tongues slide into one another's mouths before he turned his head, cheeks too hot for comfort.

How could Billy be so casual about what he was when...

Billy broke off the kiss with a loud *pop.* "Okay, then, get going. See if I care." He gave Enrique a hard spank on the ass. "But I'm gonna hold you to your promise. Next time you're in town you call me, understand?"

"*Si, si. Telefono.* You don't think I'd miss out on another night like this, do you?"

"Better not." Billy gave Enrique a push in the direction of the door. "Get back to work."

"You have to work yourself, no?"

Billy sat in a folding chair drawn up to the table, and threw Enrique a wink. "I didn't post a schedule. If there are any students waiting, they can hang on until I'm done with my breakfast."

"We finished eating."

"I didn't have dessert." Billy picked up his ever-present pack of cigarettes from the detritus of plates, half-empty glasses and saucers. He pulled out one long cylinder and lit up, exhaling a cloud of smoke. "There. Almost done."

Enrique chortled under his breath as he opened the door. "See you later, then, if you do not kill yourself with these in the meantime."

"Only the good die young, my friend. I figure I have a good sixty years left."

Shaking his head, still chuckling, Enrique headed through the door, and hopefully out of Billy's life. Billy watched him go, then turned to Quentin. "You sure do like to watch, don't you? But then again, I'm guessing after last night you like to listen, too. You're a one-man journalism team."

Quentin gave a start. He hadn't realized he'd been staring, drinking in every detail of the moving man's departure and Billy's antics. "I—I—" he stuttered.

Billy cracked up. "Come on, man, it was a joke." He glanced over the full and cluttered table, then held up a platter with some scrambled eggs. "You want the leftovers? I think they're still warm. A guy like you needs fuel for the busy, busy day I bet you've got planned." His eyes sparkled. "All that studying, making nice with the kids, studying some more, calisthenics, studying again, and maybe finishing up with half a slice of bread and a glass of water. Least I can do is see you get a good start to the day." He took another drag on his cigarette. "Aw, shit. I forgot to open the window again. Here, let me take care of that." He stood, still in nothing but his jockey shorts, and headed for the small kitchen window.

"No! I mean...no. It's quite all right. I've lived through a day and night of your incessant smoking. There's no time for pretending it's not choking me now." Quentin's temper was rising again despite his determination not to let Billy know he'd gotten to him. "Just...go back to your breakfast. Dessert. All I want is a bowl of cereal and I'll be on my way. You can go back to doing whatever you want."

"Nah. Once I finish this, I've gotta get dressed and head down to the faculty building myself. We could walk together."

"Thank you, but no. I prefer to walk alone."

"I bet you do." Billy sounded both amused and derisive.

Blast his smug hide.

As Quentin busied himself with finding a bowl and a spoon, he could feel the weight of Billy's gaze drinking him in from the top of his head to the bottom of his sensible Oxford shoes. "You do a lot of walking alone, Q?"

"I hardly see how that's your affair." Quentin hunted around for his cereal and finally found it stuffed behind three grapefruits and two boxes of powdered milk. "What did I tell you about putting fruit in the cupboards, Billy?"

"Geez, don't get your panties in a bunch. I always kept the fruit put up when I had my own place. But hey, if it bothers you, I'll take it all out. Make a nice bowl for the middle of this table." Billy tapped the littered surface. "Would that bring you happiness and joy?"

"It would be a start." Quentin poured his cereal into the bowl, headed for the refrigerator and took out what had been a full gallon of milk. At the moment, it was decidedly on the half-empty side. Weighing the container in one hand, he glared at Billy.

Billy grinned back at him. "Oops. But hey, no worries. I'll buy another jug when I'm down in the city later on."

"I see." Quentin poured a measured amount of milk over his Grape-Nuts. Not too little and not too much. Capping the container, he put it back where it belonged. Even if he had to push a partially filled glass of pop and an apple with two bites in it out of the way. Milk belonged on the second shelf, not the first, where it could be easily reached.

57

Billy would just have to learn these things. They wouldn't be able to live together otherwise.

Heat and color flooded Quentin's face again as he thought about the implications. Here he was in an apartment with a flamboyantly gay man, not only one who'd kissed him but who'd just sent an impromptu lover off after a night's wild fucking. He lived with Billy. Lived with him. One could read all sorts of things into the situation.

He refused to think about how, at one time, sharing living space with a man like Billy would have been his dream.

The man seemed in fine good humor as Quentin approached the table. He shuffled flatware and mugs out of the way, clearing a space for Quentin's bowl. "Health-food cereal. Why am I not surprised? A guy like you would never go for the Fruity Pebbles."

"I think there's enough fruit in this house already." Quentin sat down and dipped his spoon into his bowl.

He'd just taken one measured bite when Billy leaned back, exhaled a cloud of smoke and said, "So what did you think about last night?"

Quentin nearly choked.

"Seriously, man," Billy went on, oblivious to Quentin's struggle and fit of coughing. "Enrique. I love a man with caramel skin. Never been disappointed. Italian men make the best lovers. This guy, though, he was a close second. A prick like you would not believe and he knew how to use it, too."

Quentin managed to swallow. "Billy, please. I don't need to know the sordid details of your sex life."

"No? Figured it might loosen you up a little. You have, what, a girlfriend, right? You never shared morning-afters with someone?" Billy tapped the tabletop with a fork, making the tines dance along the edge of a plate. "Come on, you have to have done it one time or another."

"No. I respect Melissa's privacy, as she respects my own." Quentin took another bite of cereal and chewed determinedly. "I won't be giving you any details."

"That's a shame, man. Nothing like bonding over the way you bounced the springs." Billy hummed with seeming contentment. "Enrique, now, he talked to me about his past lovers. You know he got it on once in the back of his truck with a Texan he'd just helped move onto a ranch? Ride 'em, cowboy. He said I beat that guy by an inch."

"An inch of what?" Quentin asked before he could stop himself. Billy whooped and slapped Quentin on the leg as Quentin closed his eyes in embarrassment. "I see."

"Hey, if you've got it, flaunt it, that's what I say." Billy crushed out his cigarette and lit a second one. "You mind if I stick around? We're walking to the faculty building together, after all."

"We are not," Quentin repeated, snapping out the words. "Don't play games with me. And for the record, Dr. Jennings, I have no interest in being friends with you. It seems I need to repeat myself on this point. We share living space, but that is where things end."

"Nah. You live with someone, you've gotta get to know them." Billy made an expansive gesture with his cigarette. "You'll love me in a while. I have a way with people."

"So I've seen."

"Nah, nah, not like that." Billy was utterly unsquashable. "I mean I get under people's skin, or so I've been told. Lots of people hate me when they first meet me." He twinkled with good humor. "I win 'em over, though. Never met someone I didn't get along with sooner or later."

"I'm afraid you're out of luck this time." Quentin scooped up the last spoonful of cereal. "And I'm not waiting for you. As soon as I've rinsed this out, I'll be on my way. *Alone.*"

"Okay, fine, so you hate me right now. I'm a big boy."

"So I've seen."

"I can cope." Billy leaned back. "So why don't you get it all off your chest? Tear me a new one. You'll feel better. Go ahead and tell me what you'd like to do with me. A good punch in the nose? Uppercut to the jaw? Fist to the stomach?"

"I'm not inclined to violence." Quentin stood to carry his dish to the sink, focused on rinsing it out. "I do suggest that you clear away your mess before ants discover a feast, however."

"Shit, we have ants?" Billy sat up straighter and looked around himself. "I don't see any."

"Hypothetical ants!" Quentin barked. He turned on the faucet with a vicious jerk. "You take the least important things as if they were the most serious, and when it's something that counts—"

"Okay, cool. Now we're getting somewhere." Billy leaned back again. Quentin couldn't help turning to look at the man. He sat spraddle-legged in his chair, knees wide apart, exposing muscled thighs and strong calves, a defined chest and...and...

Quentin tore his gaze away from what Billy carried between his legs. He couldn't look. Shouldn't. Wouldn't. "I am going to clean up after myself," he said through teeth that were nearly gritted shut, "and then I am going to work. I suggest you do the same."

"There's time."

"There is not enough time!" Quentin slammed his bowl into the bottom of the sink. "Dr. Jennings, you clearly lack a sense of what matters in life."

"See, that's where we have a difference of opinion. I think that the small things are what count. Every little crumb that goes into making a day isn't just a crumb, it's a feast. Pounce on every little morsel and enjoy it with all your might. That's what makes a good life. Anything else is just going through the motions."

Quentin pinched the bridge of his nose to try and ward off an impending headache. This wasn't going to work. He and Billy had no chance of getting along at all.

"Go ahead," Billy encouraged. "Even if you don't say it out loud, think about what you'd like to do with me."

Force you to wear a tie and be in your office at the start of the day. Have you close the bathroom door while you're inside. Clean up the mess you've made. Eat healthily and sensibly.

Kiss me again.

Run your fingers through my hair.

Press your body close to mine.

Lie on your back while I'm between your legs, with your hands holding on tight...

Quentin drew in a deep, shocked breath and opened his eyes. Billy sat with his head tilted to one side, looking at Quentin as if he could read his mind. "See?" he asked softly. "The imagination's not such a bad thing, is it?"

He tried to struggle for words, but none would come. He'd slipped. God help him, he'd lost his footing. And he couldn't even go to Melissa with advice on this. If she so much as suspected he'd once again harbored lewd thoughts about a man, she'd lash him with words and then leave him high and dry.

"Please," he said, fighting against a flood of emotion. "Don't. Just don't. Dr. Jennings, I can't go on like this."

"It's Billy. And you're Quentin. Q. Q-man. Oh, wait. Maybe Quinn?"

"Quentin."

"Quinn," Billy crooned. "I bet you were Quinn somewhere in your life." Billy stood. Before Quentin could react, he'd crossed the small kitchen in a few steps and invaded Quentin's personal space, almost touching him.

Quentin felt his throat constricting with terror. Quinn. His now-hated nickname. What he'd been called in the bad old days. Oh, God. Was this some sort of divine punishment, to be taunted by such a reminder of his past? Were his convictions failing or his barriers falling?

"Go on," Billy urged. "Tell me what you want to do with me."

Lie on my stomach while you smooth oil down my back and dip between the...

Oh, God.

"I don't want anything to do with you," Quentin protested.

"See, that's where I think you're wrong. I think you want to have a lot to do with me." Billy reached up and traced a line down Quentin's cheek. "I'm not new at this. I can see the hunger in a man's eyes. The need. You say you have a girlfriend, but you're burning up inside. Burning and drowning. You know what you want, even if you won't admit it to yourself."

Quentin felt himself losing ground. "Billy...I..."

"Shh. Hush, baby, hush. Just let me make you feel good."

"Billy..."

"I like it when you say my name like that. Makes me feel like I've got a hope here." Billy's gaze had turned warm. He tossed his cigarette into the sink. "Stand still for just a second, Quinn."

Quentin made one last effort. "Why should I?"

"Because I'm about to do this." Billy moved in quickly and pressed his lips to Quentin's for the second time in as many days. He tasted of salt and smoke and coffee. His lips were the softest Quentin had ever felt, even more so than Melissa's. There was no tang of lipstick to get past. Just honest, male flavor and bitter ash.

Quentin moaned and sagged against the kitchen counter. Billy seemed to take this as a sign of interest and nestled in tighter, putting one hand on Quentin's hip and pressing the other to his back. He increased the pressure on Quentin's mouth, flicking his tongue at the seam of Quentin's lips.

With a whimper of despair, Quentin opened up to let Billy inside. The man's tongue was nimble and quick, darting inside like a firefly that left a glow in its wake. He traced the line of Quentin's own tongue, then tangled them together. Slowly, he tilted their heads for better, deeper access.

Quentin felt his own hands itching to cradle Billy. He couldn't seem to help or stop himself. All the old urges, the desires, the *needs,* every one of them were flooding back in. He couldn't stop the pull. All he could do was surrender to the tide.

When Billy shifted back, Quentin, God help him, almost tugged the man close again. "There," Billy said, licking his lips. "I think that's what you want to do with me. Hypothesis confirmed."

Quentin's hand flew to his mouth. He could hear the water running, his heart beating and the sound of his own breath coming in quick gasps. A buzzing began and started to take over his head. "No," he protested. "No. I don't do this anymore. I'm straight now. I can't. So many people would be disappointed—"

"What matters more? Them, or being true to yourself?"

"I can't. Don't make me do this." Quentin tore away from Billy's arms. Ignoring his dish in the sink, pushing past Billy, he headed for the front door. "Leave me alone, please," he said, knowing it was begging, but not caring. "Billy, I can't do this."

"You could if you'd let yourself. What's so wrong about being this way?"

"It's not my path anymore. It's wrong. I won't. I swore." Quentin wrenched the door open. "Goodbye, Dr. Jennings."

With that, he fled out onto the porch, clattering down the stairs and onto the track. By the time he hit the trail, he was running fast as he could, not caring about how he might ruin his outfit with sweat.

The biggest problem was that he knew no matter how hard he ran, he'd never be able to leave this behind. It would haunt him all day wherever he turned.

And worst of all, it was his own fault, wasn't it?

Chapter Five

"No, no. It's far too early to be worrying about the midterm." Quentin attempted a reassuring smile. He had a distinct feeling that it came out more like a twisted grimace. The look of doubt on the student's face confirmed his hypothesis. He tried again, with mixed results. "The results on this quiz are disappointing, but simply because I know you can do better."

The student frowned. "You don't even know my name."

"Of course I do. Eleanor, isn't it?"

"Alisha."

"Oh. Oh, I see. My apologies, Alisha." Quentin fumbled through his seating chart for the girl's class, the paper kept close at hand so he could sneak peeks whenever students came by. His mind was so often jammed full of lesson plans and mental notes he couldn't always put a name to a face, and it wouldn't do if Ten Hawks found out he was so uninformed about his students. Running his finger down the rows, he frowned. Blonde hair, mostly in a ponytail, frequently seen in a hoodie...

The girl seemed amused by his confusion. "Take it easy. You were right. It's Eleanor. I was just testing you. Seeing if you were on your toes."

"Unless you want your professor to have a heart attack while he's counseling you, I suggest you don't test me again," Quentin said dryly. "Now, Eleanor—"

"Elly, actually. And come on, lighten up a little." The student grinned in a way that reminded Quentin of Billy. Teasing, mischievous. A little too daring for her own good. Quentin starred her name in the seating chart, a designation that meant "possible trouble".

Ten Hawks hadn't been joking about how Sweetwater was under funded. He had an office, to be sure, but it was hardly larger than a broom closet. His work computer was refurbished, and the chairs had definitely seen hard use. The one he sat in squeaked if he moved too quickly. Eleanor's seat had scarred wooden arms.

Eleanor lifted her hands in surrender. "Okay, that was pushing. I'm sorry. But look, about that quiz. I wasn't prepared that day."

"That is more or less the point of a pop quiz."

"Yeah, but if you'd mentioned that we should study the Victorian era in general, I might have boned up on it a little. Hey, you okay?"

Quentin broke the lead off his pencil.

Eleanor eyed him warily as if wondering about Quentin's own potential for snapping. "I'm just saying you could have given us some hints about the material on the quiz, that's all."

"I see. Would you prefer no surprise tests of any kind, then? Do you know if the rest of the class feels the same way?" From the quiz scores, none above a B minus, Quentin suspected that would be the case. But honestly, if they'd been paying attention at all, they should have picked up on his not-so-subtle cues that they would have impromptu checks on their progress. He'd even put it in the syllabus.

"For sure." Eleanor seemed to relax. She sat back a little in her chair with the boneless grace of the young and slim. "Give us some time to prepare. We've got lives outside your class, you know? I'm in American Lit with Dr. Jennings, and he always warns us the night before."

"I see," Quentin said tightly. "That surprises me. I'd have thought Dr. Jennings would be more spontaneous."

"Oh, he's a hella hoot in class. Oops, sorry about the language. He throws out questions, and if you answer them right you get a point. Ten points gets you one grade up on the next quiz. It's fun. Maybe you should try it."

Quentin's grip tightened on his pencil. "If I were exactly like Dr. Jennings, there would hardly be a difference between the two classes, now would there?"

"Outside of the continent and the historical era? But oh, yeah, Dr. Jennings. He's so cool." Eleanor winked and wound a strand of honey-blonde hair around one finger. "Half the girls have a crush on him. Some of the guys, too."

"Eleanor, that's hardly appropriate. What Dr. Jennings does or does not do, or the number of lovesick students he has, has no influence on this meeting whatsoever. We met to discuss a grade you believed was unfair." Quentin picked up Eleanor's paper with the neat C minus written in red ink on the upper left-hand corner. "You claim that with preparation you can do better?"

"Absolutely. So you'll warn us next time?"

Quentin gave up. "Yes, I will. Now, did you need anything else?"

"Nope. I gotta get to Dr. Jennings' office next. He's helping me out with some early Twain. Did you know MT was friends with Emperor Norton?"

"I had no idea." The pencil began to creak in protest under Quentin's punishing grip. "Is this the sort of thing Dr. Jennings teaches you?"

"Oh, yeah. He throws in all sorts of fun stuff." Eleanor stood and shrugged on her backpack. "Thanks for the meeting. I'll see you in class."

"Eleanor..."

"Yeah?" She cocked one hip as she looked at him. God, all the child needed was a wad of bubble gum to chew on and she'd be back in high school again. When did undergraduates get so young? "Is there something else?"

"I think that would be my question. And I simply wanted to let you know that I don't enjoy being so informal. I would like for my students to respect me as well."

Eleanor raised an eyebrow, but nodded. "Okay. Sorry. Can I go now? Dr. Jennings is gonna be waiting."

"Yes, yes. Go." Quentin waved her off with his pencil.

"Thanks. You live with him, right? I'm pushing again, but I gotta know. Is he as much fun when he's off the clock?"

Quentin's pencil snapped in half in his hand. "I said you could go, Eleanor. Or do you want an impromptu essay assigned on the Victorian era?"

"Whoa, whoa, no. I'm out of here." Eleanor backed out of his office. "See you in class, Prof."

"Don't address me as—"

But she was gone.

Quentin looked at the ragged halves of his pencil and heaved a sigh. He threw them down on his desk, where one fragment rolled off onto the floor and the other seated itself in the middle of his desk chart. Leaning forward, he put his head into his hands and closed his eyes.

"Problems?"

The voice startled Quentin into sitting back up again, searching for the source of the question. If anyone caught him in a moment of despair it could be disastrous. He relaxed, but only a little, when he saw that it was just Andy, leaning against the frame of his door with both hands stuffed in his pockets.

"Andy. Hello." Quentin tried for another smile, but felt that this one came out distinctly pale. "Come in if you have the time." Truth be told, he felt like being alone, but it wouldn't do to alienate one of the few professors who had shown him some degree of friendship. This wouldn't be the first time Andy had stopped by for a chat. Ever so slowly, Quentin was developing a feeling that he could trust the man. He was even beginning to like him. "I'm afraid I don't have anything to offer you."

"And here I was hoping to steal the apple from teacher's desk." Andy winked as he sauntered in. Instead of taking a seat, however, he stood at Quentin's side and put a hand on his shoulder. Quentin stiffened as the man's fingers began to massage taut muscles. "I couldn't help overhearing, just a little, about the way you were talking to that student."

"Eavesdropping, you mean," Quentin said without thinking. "Oh. Oh, I'm sorry. I meant to say—"

Andy laughed without malice. "Maybe eavesdropping a little. You might want to go easier on the students. Ten Hawks likes his professors to be relaxed, easy to approach."

"I was hardly an ogre," Quentin protested.

"No. Just a stuffed shirt." Andy kept on massaging Quentin's shoulders. The warmth of his hand seeped through the thin cotton of Quentin's shirt and felt as if it were leaving a mark on his skin. Quentin closed his eyes, struggling hard against the sensations that threatened to overwhelm him.

"God, you're tense," Andy remarked in mild disapproval. "Hard as a board."

"I'm quite all right, thank you."

"Well, there's a lie." Andy removed his hand at last. "You know what a man like you needs?"

Quentin dreaded the answer. "What?"

"A little bit of R & R, that's what. How about you and I go down into the town and hit a bar? A good local beer would go a long way toward calming you down."

The request was nothing new. Andy had been trying to coax Quentin out of his office for weeks. "It's barely past noon."

"Ah, hell, it's five o'clock somewhere." Andy ran his finger down the curve of Quentin's shoulder, leaving a heat trail in his wake. "Come on, what do you say? You and me, off to have a quiet drink someplace. You can tell me about what's bothering you."

A sudden suspicion blossomed. "Did Ten Hawks put you up to this?"

"Ben? Hell, no. He's been buried in a stack of letters to students for a few days now. He likes to send out notes of encouragement. Adds a five-dollar gift certificate to the student café, too." Andy tilted his head to one side. "Now there's a thought. If you don't feel like a bar, how about a coffee shop? I know a great place in the town. Not exactly a tearoom, what with the abstract art and all, but it should be mostly empty around this time of day."

"Hardly surprising, given that morning and the proper time for coffee are well past."

"Jeez, you only drink java in the morning? I couldn't live without at least one cup an hour."

"That," Quentin remarked dryly, "explains a lot about your perpetually wired personality. Thank you, Andy, but truly, I couldn't. I still have a stack of papers to grade."

"They'll be here when we get back. And from what I hear, you're not too crazy about going home these days."

Quentin snapped his head up so fast his neck twinged in protest, staring at Andy. "Who—I—where did you hear this rumor?"

Andy shrugged. "Well, you're living with Billy, right? He's not exactly one to keep his mouth shut about things. Come on, a nice walk and a cup of coffee will do you a world of good."

Quentin's thoughts raced. If he didn't go with Andy, what could happen? Would word get out that he was unfriendly and didn't enjoy socializing with his peers? That would no doubt bring Ten Hawks down to his office for a good-natured scolding. Between the prospect of such a visit and the prospect of missed work time, it seemed like the devil's choice. But could he afford not to go?

"Very well," he relented, closing his grade book and standing. "We'll go and have a cup of coffee. Just one, though, if you don't mind."

"And decaf, right?" Andy chuckled. "You might want to take that overshirt off. It's warm enough outside to start sweating."

Quentin hesitated. Unless he was jogging, he hated to get overheated. Sweatiness led to smelliness, and then he'd need a shower before he could get back to work. "On second thought, Andy..."

"Say no more. I've got an illicit coffeemaker in my office. I'll just go and grab a couple of mugs, and I'll be right back. We can take our break in here." He patted the back of Quentin's chair. "To be frank, my friend, you look like a man with more than a few troubles. You need a listening ear, and I swear I won't tell a soul. You can trust me."

Trust. The key word. Quentin felt something click inside him, like tumblers working inside a lock. His chest tightened at the same time that his heart relaxed. "You do promise?"

"On my life." Andy lifted his hand. "Just a few seconds for that coffee to come right up. You sit tight."

Quentin didn't think he could sit any other way. His hands felt for the armrests to his chair, one of them patched up with black duct tape, and gripped hard. He heard Andy leave, rather than watching him go, and waited for the man to return with his pulse thudding in his throat. *Trust.* Did he really dare trust Andy with the whole of what was bothering him? The man had proved himself to be a reliable sort so far...

"Here we are." Andy reappeared with two mugs in hand. He offered Quentin one with a plain Sweetwater logo, and kept one decorated with Einstein's equation for himself. He shut the door behind himself, and sat in the empty guest chair. "Now. Drink up, and tell me what's on your mind. Confession's good for the soul."

Father Andrew had said much the same thing. If he dared in the here and now...

Quentin swallowed uneasily, then took a sip of his coffee. It tasted burned, as if it had been cooking for a while, but cream and sugar went a good ways toward disguising the bitterness. "Thank you," he said as he took another sip. The brew warmed his insides as it went down, much better than any beer would have. "Confessions. Well, now..."

Andy leaned forward. "Come on, man, out with it. I'm not the only one who's noticed how tense you are. Let it all go, and then maybe you'll feel better."

"You're so sure of that?"

"Well." Andy shrugged. "We won't know until you try, will we?"

His attitude of patient waiting reminded Quentin so strongly of meetings with Father Andrew that the inclination to talk became almost too tempting to resist. He took a third sip of coffee and put his mug down, afraid his fingers would begin shaking. "Do you promise that you won't repeat this to anyone?" he asked, not looking at Andy. Eye contact would make this ordeal all the more uncomfortable.

"Cross my heart."

"All right, then." Quentin picked up one of his broken pencil halves and began to play with the thing, turning it over and over in his fingers. Focusing on an inanimate object helped one to be frank in their speech. He didn't know why it worked. Perhaps the habit was particular to himself. "The problem is...Dr. Jennings."

"Billy, you mean."

"Billy," Quentin acknowledged. "He's rather more unorthodox than Dr. Ten Hawks would have led me to believe."

"Ten Hawks gets a little het up if you don't call him just plain Ten Hawks. That, or Ben."

Was that a warning? Quentin tried to relax his muscles. "Very well. Ten Hawks. He told me that Billy was...but he's so much more. He's...flamboyant. Outrageous."

"Billy can be a handful, all right."

Quentin flashed briefly on a fantasy of his own hand cupping one of Billy's tight ass cheeks. His face grew hot and he deliberately pricked a finger with the broken pencil. The slight stab of pain brought him back to himself. "He is, in a nutshell, a slob, inconsiderate, and unabashedly, promiscuously homosexual. I'm not certain how much longer he and I can continue to share accommodations."

"Huh." Andy sounded as if he were frowning. "Is it the gay thing you're having a problem with? Because I have to tell you, that's a bit homophobic. I'm more or less tilted in that direction myself. I still like the ladies, mind you, but I don't say no to a fine man when he wants to spend a little time with me."

Quentin didn't want to offend Andy, even if he was recoiling from the man's casual words. He chose his phrases with care. "My problem is with the whole of Billy and the way he comports himself. His blatant disregard for any consideration on my behalf. I don't want to..." Quentin trailed off.

"Can't stand him flaunting himself about, then?"

Quentin nodded.

"You need to grow a thicker skin," Andy said bluntly. "I'm not saying living with a man like Billy is going to be easy in any case, but—"

"I used to be gay," Quentin blurted. He regretted the words the second they flew out of his mouth, but there was nothing to be done about them at that point. He gritted his teeth and waited for Andy's reaction.

It wasn't what he'd expected. No recriminations, but honest concern instead. "Used to be? What d'you mean?" The man leaned forward, as if he were truly compassionate. Once again, Quentin was reminded of his personal counselor. It would be so easy to trust.

Perhaps too easy. "Once upon a time, in my misspent youth, I believed myself to be gay. I'd spent my adolescent years torn between admiring males and females, and after spending time with a certain young man I decided that I was gay."

"Uh-huh. And what happened then?"

"Oh, I was happy as a lark. For a time. One young man led to another. I eventually experienced homoerotic sex, and enjoyed it very much. I became...incautious."

"You? That's hard to believe."

"Yes. Well. I wasn't always as I am now. I became quite outrageous. There was a fad at the time for young men of my kind to decorate themselves in outlandish fashions. Dyed hair, slight applications of makeup. I reveled in what I believed to be a realization of my true self."

"Sounds like you were having a good time. But you said 'used to be gay'. Something happened, then, didn't it?"

Quentin nodded. "There was...a disastrous occurrence that led me to spending some time at a rehabilitation center where I tried to understand myself. The counselors were all very kind. They guided me through the discovery that I had been lying to myself and helped me realize I preferred females and a quiet lifestyle as opposed to how I had been behaving."

"I see." Andy tapped the armrest of his chair. "Sounds a bit like one of those god-awful deprogramming hellholes, if you ask me."

"Some have described it thusly. I choose to think of that time as a turning point in my life. I put my wilder ways behind me and, with the help of intensive therapy, turned my life around. I went back to the self I had been, no adornments, and began asking females out on dates."

"Any of them light your fire, so to speak?"

Quentin tensed. "I had several pleasant encounters. I refrained from sexual intercourse, naturally, while under the Center's observation. My personal advisor disapproved of extramarital relations."

"Oh, come on, now. You're telling me you've been celibate for how many years now?"

"No," Quentin admitted. He took a sip of coffee to steady himself. "I have Melissa. She and I are exclusive to one another.

She requested sex as a part of our relationship, and after debating the issue with myself I decided to comply."

"Decided to comply. God, that's romantic."

"You don't know anything about Melissa," Quentin protested. "She's a fine, upstanding young woman with solid moral values and a bright future in front of her."

"Sounds like you're describing a star pupil."

"Not at all. I'm sure that Melissa loves me, and I'm quite fond of her. I *do* love her." Quentin put his mug down. It was half-empty, but he had no more interest in the contents. "We are all but engaged, after all. All that's lacking is a ring."

"And where is she, while you're teaching up here in the middle of nowhere? I sure as hell haven't seen her around during the past couple of months."

"She's finishing her law degree. We'll have a couple of years apart, but then we'll spend the rest of our lives together."

"Producing two-point-five children and purchasing a house with a white picket fence, no doubt." Andy drained the last of his own coffee and began toying with the mug. "Quentin...has it ever occurred to you that maybe that counselor was wrong? If you were being true to yourself when you decided you were gay, where did the mistake come in?"

Quentin shook his head. "That's irrelevant. I was misguided, and that's the end of it. All I want to do now is live a normal life."

"And gays can't have a normal life, can they?"

"I'm not saying that."

"No, but you're doing a damn fine job of implication. So, Billy's blatant about his sexuality and this bothers you. It's not his smoking, his late hours or his other habits. You can't bear living with a reminder of what you might have been without that Center and its counselors stepping in to rearrange your life. Not to mention this Melissa, who sounds like she's got you wrapped around her little finger."

"Don't impugn Melissa."

"Look, Quentin...all I'm saying is, if this is what's bothering you, then you need to take some time to think." Andy leaned forward again. He put out a hand and rested it on top of Quentin's.

Quentin pulled away automatically.

Andy didn't seem fazed. "You need to figure out what it is you truly want for yourself, no therapists involved. A man has to be true to himself and what he needs, not what others tell him. And I know that's the pot calling the kettle black, but I'm not encouraging you one way or another. I'm just saying it might be time for another self-evaluation. Figure out what you really want, whether it's this Melissa or a return to what you once thought you were."

Quentin nodded stiffly. "Thank you, Andy. I think that's all the time I have for coffee and conversation. If you don't mind, I'd like to finish grading these papers now."

Andy could, at least, take a hint. "All right, my friend. I'll take myself back to my office. But listen, any time you have an urge to talk, just stop in. I'll make time for you. Whatever you need to talk about." He moved in closer, causing Quentin's heart to skip a beat, but it was only to retrieve his coffee mug. "Any time. I mean that."

"Thank you. Please close the door on your way out."

Andy left without another word. When he was gone and the door clicked shut behind him, Quentin rested his elbows on his desk and ground the palms of his hands against his eyes.

The trouble wasn't his need for a self re-evaluation. He knew what he wanted. What he seemed to need more and more as each day living with Billy went by.

He wanted Billy. But he couldn't have the man, could he?

He shouldn't.

He wouldn't.

"Oh, God," he said softly, rocking his head back and forth. "There has to be someone who can help me. Someone who'll help me get all this out of my system, instead of a man who encourages me down the wrong path."

A thought occurred to him. Raising up, he reached for his cell phone and hit speed-dial. Four rings and straight to voice mail, but he left a message regardless, knowing she checked rigorously. "Melissa, this is Quentin. How would you feel about a weekend visit up here in the mountains? I'd love to have you see where I work... I truly have been missing you terribly..."

Chapter Six

From the moment Melissa stepped off the train platform, Quentin's heart seemed to settle back into a normal rhythm for the first time in months. She didn't notice him at first, checking her watch and then her PDA, so he had time to look at her. Drink her in.

Melissa. So beautiful. Tastefully cut clothes, large brown eyes, elegantly slim arms and legs. She'd lost a little weight...and oh. She'd cut her hair. At first Quentin had thought it was tied back in a ponytail but no, Melissa would never be that informal. It'd been cut into a short professional style, close to her head. Quentin supposed it would be easy to arrange and look proper in court, but he'd loved running his fingers through the formerly long, baby-fine locks.

Still, it didn't matter how she'd changed. She was still a gorgeous woman, one he was tremendously lucky would have him, and most important of all she was here, in Sweetwater.

Lifting her head, Melissa began to scan the crowd. Quentin didn't wave or try to attract her attention. Melissa hated a scene. Instead, he began to thread his way through the crowd of passengers getting off, trying to reach her side without undue fuss. He held the dozen roses he'd purchased close to his chest, attempting to keep them from getting crushed in the throng.

Halfway there, he felt Melissa's gaze settle on him. She had the piercing sort of look that no male or female could miss once she'd picked them out. Quentin appreciated it for the most part. He knew, with that look focused on him, he had her full attention.

Her impatient attention, but nevertheless.

Melissa didn't move from her spot on the platform, letting disembarking passengers swarm around her instead of making way. She tapped one high-heeled foot impatiently as Quentin drew closer. With a shake of her head, she stowed the PDA in her small leather pocketbook.

"Quentin," she said when he was close enough, and put out her hand. Quentin took it for a quick shake. Melissa didn't care for public displays of overt affection. However, as her hand closed over his, Quentin felt a pulse of relief so strong he impulsively reached around the woman and pulled her into a hug that squashed the roses between them.

"Stop that," Melissa said sternly, pushing him away with a firm but discreet hand. "Quentin, we're in public. If I can remember that, so can you. Don't make a spectacle of yourself where other people can see. God knows you're bad enough in private. Don't carry your shortcomings into the public eye."

"I'm—I'm sorry, Melissa." Quentin felt himself grow warm with embarrassment. "I should have known better. I'll be more careful."

"Make sure that you are." Melissa dusted off the sleeves of her smartly cut black suit. Had she come straight from her office? The last time they'd talked, Melissa was just starting to work part-time in a firm of lawyers. Nothing so grand as even clerking, but as she claimed, it was a start.

"I bought you roses," Quentin ventured, holding out the bouquet. He hadn't been able to afford an arrangement, but he thought these were rather nice. They had sprigs of baby's breath mixed among the crimson blossoms, something he'd always liked. Oh, dear, but Melissa didn't, did she?

Melissa ran a critical eye over the flowers. "These are wilting. Honestly, Quentin, can't you do anything right? Throw them away. I don't want to carry around a handful of dead roses."

"Wilting? Surely not. They're only a little brown around the edges of a few petals."

"I said wilting and I meant wilting." Melissa displayed a small flash of well-controlled anger. "Are you going to throw them away, or do I have to?" She tapped her foot again. "Well, Quentin?"

Quentin felt a brief, startling twitch of irritation. Quickly, he tamped it down. What was he thinking? "Of course. I'll take care of the problem for you." Quentin withdrew the roses and searched for the nearest trash can. He found one a few feet away and inserted his bouquet in the bin. Watching the rubbish swallow up his gift hurt a bit, but he'd survive. Only the best for Melissa. He should have known better.

When he turned back, Melissa was smiling a tight little smile. "I hope you at least have a taxi waiting. It's colder up here than you led me to believe. I have no desire to catch some sort of bug while waiting for someone vacant to pull up. Coming up here for a night has already taken up a valuable piece of my time, and I can't afford any more off the job."

"Actually," Quentin ventured, "I've borrowed a car. A fellow professor, Andy, lent me his vehicle so that we wouldn't have to pay for a taxi."

"*We* pay for a taxi? Have you forgotten your manners? And what kind of professor lends out his car on a whim?"

"He and I are friends, of a sort..."

"Really?" Melissa raised one sculpted eyebrow. "I'll have to meet him while I'm here. I don't want you associating with any bad influences. I have enough trouble keeping you on the straight and narrow without someone in your life to lure you off the path."

Quentin thought briefly of Billy and winced internally. He'd never complained to Melissa about his roommate, but wondered now if he should have. She'd be likely to have a fit when she met the charismatic chain-smoker, rather than being charmed by him. Billy's ability to make friends seemed effortless with everyone else, but Quentin had the feeling that putting Melissa and Billy in the same room together would have the same effect as tossing a lit match into a puddle of gasoline.

Not that Melissa would be anything but coldly polite to Billy. The explosion would come later, when she was alone with Quentin. *Never air your dirty laundry in public.*

"Go and get my suitcase," Melissa directed. "It's the Vuitton in charcoal. There should be a claim tag attached so you won't mix it up with anyone else's things. Do be careful this time."

Quentin nodded, accepting the criticism. He'd picked up the wrong bag once after a short flight from Charlotte to Raleigh when he'd accompanied Melissa to a conference, and she'd been...ill pleased. Giving her a tentative smile, he headed off to the spot where burly men were shifting cases out of the luggage compartments. As he went, he saw Melissa pull out a slimline cell phone and hit a button.

"Yes, Charles? I've arrived. No, there's no need for worry. Quentin's here to pick me up. Now, Charles, don't concern yourself. Quentin can get me to a hotel in one piece. Charles, I don't like your tone of voice..."

Quentin frowned to himself. Charles? Melissa had never mentioned a Charles before. Well, he probably worked at the same firm that she did. It was good of the partners or employees to take an interest in her well-being. He liked knowing that there were others to take care of Melissa when he wasn't with her.

Not, of course, that she needed looking after. Melissa was a force to be reckoned with under any circumstances.

Reaching the baggage drop, Quentin waited patiently. He wouldn't know Vuitton from Samsonite, but he was familiar with Melissa's tastes. When a charcoal suitcase came off, along with a dress bag, both spanking new, he pushed forward a little to claim them.

The baggage handler stopped him with a look. "You don't look like any Melissa Rife to me."

Quentin blinked. "No. No, of course not. She's sent me to pick up her belongings while she checks in with her home office."

"Got some ID?" The heavyset man spat out a gobbet of tobacco juice and waited, hands on his hips. Melissa's dress bag slithered down into a heap. "She's got it on here that a Quentin Whiteside can get her things, no one else. And let me tell you, after the hell that finicky ice bitch put us through on the ride up here, I'm not about to get her pissed off again."

"ID, of course." Quentin reached for his wallet and withdrew his driver's license. It was close to expiry, but it should still be sufficient. Passing it over, he waited for the handler to make his judgment. He did hope that the man would let him take the baggage. He didn't want to raise Melissa's ire by asking her for help.

She didn't like it when he wasn't self-sufficient.

The handler studied Quentin's license. "You've lost a hell of a lot of weight," he said, but passed it back. "Okay, you can take this shit. Be careful. It's heavy as fuck."

"Thank you." Quentin pushed card into wallet and wallet into neatly pressed trousers. Billy had made such fun of him for ironing a pair of chinos, but he hoped Melissa would be satisfied with his efforts. She hadn't criticized him for his clothing choice, at least. "Excuse me." The man didn't seem inclined to help, so Quentin picked up Melissa's luggage by himself. His knees nearly buckled. Good heavens, what did she have in her suitcase? Bricks?

Melissa's foot was tapping again by the time Quentin made his way back to her. "You didn't miss the dress bag," she approved. "Well done."

Quentin beamed.

"You could have warned me that it would be this chilly up here, though." Melissa frowned slightly. "Approximately fifty degrees is cold, Quentin. I'm dressed for a warmer climate. Give me your jacket."

"Of course." Quentin put down the luggage, shrugged out of his warmly lined coat, and helped Melissa into the garment.

She wrinkled her nose. "This smells like cigarette smoke. Quentin, have you been indulging in tobacco? I realize you used to smoke back in your younger days, but if you've started up again we really need to have a talk."

"Me? Oh, no. No. This is...my roommate..."

"I see. You're sharing accommodations with a smoker." Melissa heaved a sigh. "Well, I certainly hope you don't expect me to stay in the same space as him tonight. Smoke makes me cough."

"I know. I mean, no, you won't be staying in the faculty lodging tonight." Quentin tried a smile. "I've reserved a room at the Sweetwater Bed and Breakfast. It's a queen-sized bed in case I might be able to stay—"

"We'll see." Melissa aimed a pointed gaze at the luggage. Quentin hastily picked the bags back up. "All right. Where is this car? And really, Quentin, the next time you want to see me with so little notice, I would appreciate not having to travel by train. Wait until we have enough saved for a plane ticket."

"It's only a few hundred miles."

"Are you correcting me?"

"Of course not. I apologize for the uncomfortable mode of travel."

Melissa's gimlet stare was beginning to make Quentin uneasy. He felt, uncomfortably, as if he'd failed her yet again.

Quentin cleared his throat. "The car is much more comfortable, although I'm afraid it's not the latest make or model. I had to take what I could get, you see, and it was kind of Andy to offer his vehicle on loan."

"Andy? So you're on first-name terms with your fellow professors?"

"With him, at least. He's become something of a friend, as I said."

"A confidante? Quentin, I do hope you haven't been spreading gossip around. I'll talk with this Andy and see if you've been telling tales out of school, so to speak. Will we meet him tonight?"

Quentin desperately hoped that Andy could be a good liar. He shook his head. "I don't have to return the car before tomorrow. He said I could keep it overnight."

"Then let's get out of the cold." Even though she was wrapped in Quentin's coat and should have been toasty warm, Melissa gave a small shiver. "I really can't afford to catch anything, Quentin."

"No, of course not." Quentin arranged the luggage in his left hand and offered Melissa his right arm. "Allow me?"

Melissa gave him a dubious look but did place her hand on his elbow. "No more liberties," she warned him. "This is as far as I want to go in public."

Quentin felt that surge of aggravation well up again. For heaven's sake, they were all but engaged. "I'll be careful," was all he chose to say. "Now, if you'll follow me to the parking lot, it's the red Corolla parked over by a light pole. Just to our left there. Do you see it?"

Melissa stopped. A frown curved down the corners of her mouth. "Rust-red, you mean. Wholly unacceptable. Quentin, call us a taxi. I won't travel in something like that. It looks like it's held together with duct tape."

Quentin's heart sank. If Melissa wouldn't accept the ride, he'd have to spend still more money he could hardly spare to get a cab back to pick up Andy's car. "I did warn you."

"Are you correcting me again?" Melissa demanded.

Quentin gave up. "No, Melissa. I'll go and call for a taxi. Why don't you wait inside the station where it's warm?"

"I'll do that. Don't disappoint me again." Still wearing his coat, Melissa clicked off on her heels toward the station. Quentin gazed after her, then sighed. He reached into his pocket for some loose change, hopefully enough to make a phone call.

He'd missed Melissa so much, but it seemed that he could do nothing right. He'd just have to try harder. He *needed* Melissa.

Even if he couldn't tell her exactly why.

CRCBEO

"This is it? This is where you live? Really, Quentin, you should have said something or at least tried to find better accommodations." Melissa gazed at the faculty housing with a critical eye. "Driver, wait here. I don't think we'll be long." She turned away before she could catch the taxi man giving her the finger, for which Quentin was devoutly grateful. "This place is on the verge of being condemned. What is the administration thinking?"

Quentin blinked. "It's a perfectly serviceable building," he said without thinking. "I've been quite comfortable here."

"And you're correcting me again." Melissa reached into her pocketbook and pulled out her cell phone. "We'll have to work on your manners, Quentin. You've backslidden so far since we last met. I wondered why you needed to see me in such a hurry. Do you realize I left important work unfinished to come up and visit you? Go ahead and get the door unlocked. I'll just make a quick call."

"The reception isn't spectacular up here—"

"I think I can handle myself." Melissa clicked the phone open and hit a speed-dial button. "Hello, Charles? Yes, I'm still fine. We're at the housing right now, but hopefully not for long. The McClark case? You should find my notes on the corner of my desk in the out tray. Of course I finished up before I left..."

Quentin ducked his head and reached for the small set of keys in his pocket. A racket from within caught his attention, causing him to frown in confusion. After eight p.m. the outer door was locked by campus security. But if no one but faculty were supposed to be in there, then why did he hear a commotion?

Oh, dear Lord, was someone holding a party?

He stiffened. *Billy*. God, no.

Hurrying through his unlocking, Quentin turned back to Melissa. "Perhaps you'd rather not come in," he ventured. "My roommate is a little messy from time to time and it might be best if you don't see this."

"Not come in?" Melissa disconnected her call. She gave Quentin what might have been a scowl on a less polished face. "I do plan to come in. I'll need to see what your living conditions are like, after all. Regardless of how your roommate behaves, I want to see your private quarters. I expect you to have remembered how to keep order."

As if he were a child.

God, why am I getting angry? This is just Melissa...being Melissa.

"Give me a moment first?" Quentin begged—no, requested. "I'll just be sure that there isn't any company visiting."

"Why would there be company this late at night? What are you hiding from me?" Melissa strode up to join him at the door. "Go ahead. I want to see what you're keeping a secret."

"Nothing. I swear."

"Then you have nothing to risk by letting me in, do you?" Melissa folded her arms across her chest. "Open the door. Now."

Swallowing hard, Quentin turned the lock. He stood aside for Melissa to enter first, pushing the door open for her. She tsked. "No magnetized keycards. Honestly, anyone could just use a credit card and break in here. It's a good thing you don't have anything valuable. And really, what *is* that racket?" She pointed at his door. "Do you have noisy neighbors? How are you expected to get any work done?" The cell phone came out again. "Give me the number for the campus police."

"Melissa, please don't. I'm afraid..." Quentin swallowed. "Well, this is where I live. I did warn you about my roommate."

Melissa drew back as if she'd touched something dirty. "I see. We certainly will have to work on finding you a more suitable living place."

"There's really nothing unless you go down into the town, and it's a two-mile walk uphill from there."

"Quentin," Melissa warned. "Contradict me one more time and I'll expect an immediate ride back to the train station. I didn't come down here to have you cross me at every turn."

"Yes, Melissa." Quentin hesitated. "Do you still want to come in?"

His prayer that she wouldn't was denied. "Of course I do. I intend to have a few words with your so-called roommate. He needs to understand some things about respect, silence and professional behavior." Melissa's eyes glowed with anticipation. "Just point him out to me once we're inside."

Oh, God. Good luck. Heaven help me.

Nervously, Quentin inserted his key into the apartment lock. The door vibrated a little with the sound of the music booming from within. Truth be told, he'd gotten used to Billy's fondness for foot-long woofers, but when Melissa saw...

The door swung open onto a veritable swarm of people. Students. They milled around in groups, laughing and chattering amongst themselves. Almost every one of them held a plastic cup of some sort. Quentin smelled beer and ginger ale on the air, as well as the ever-present cigarette smoke.

"Billy?" he called over the din. "Billy, please come out. I'd like for you to meet someone."

"Yeah, yeah, I'm on my way," Billy shouted back from the kitchen. He emerged with cigarette clasped between his lips, both hands full of beverages. Putting them down on an end table—without coasters—he took his cigarette and inhaled deeply. "Quinn." His grin was infectious and charming as ever as he used the nickname he didn't know held so many unwelcome—yes, unwelcome—reminders of the past. "Who'd *you* bring home? Don't tell me you've got a date."

Melissa stood solidly still at Quentin's elbow. He didn't turn around to face her, afraid of the look likely to be on her face. "This is Melissa, the woman who I hope will become my fiancée. Melissa, this is, well, Billy. Dr. Jennings. My roommate."

"I see." Melissa's voice was chillier than the outside air. "And is this how you normally spend your evenings, Billy?"

"What, this?" Billy waved around himself. "Nah. This is the wind-down after study group."

"And what are you studying? Advanced courses in how to be a hoodlum?"

Billy cracked up. "Oh, yeah. She's a pistol. Watch out how you squeeze that trigger, Quinn. She'll go off and *boom.* Come on in. Just watch where you walk."

Melissa withdrew a couple of steps, obviously revising her plan when weighed against the current parameters. "I'll stay outside, thank you. But tomorrow, before I leave, you and I will have a talk, Professor."

"Call me Billy."

"I'll call you Professor, thank you."

"Geez, make me feel old, why don't you? It's Billy to my friends, but if you insist, it's Dr. Jennings." Billy threw a wink at his crowd. "Not that anyone else here wants to be formal, right?"

A cheer went up. Melissa grew stiller and colder. "I see. Quentin, get your things. We won't be staying here any longer than it takes for you to pack a bag. Pick up whatever clothes you need as well as your books. I've brought some of my own. We can study tonight before bed."

"Might I suggest that you wait on the porch where the air is fresher? I know how the smell of tobacco bothers you, after all." And really, the smoke was thick enough to make Quentin, who'd gotten used to the odor, want to cough. His eyes stung. "I won't be a minute."

"I'll expect you to hurry." Melissa clicked out onto the porch, reaching for her cell phone. "Charles? Really, this is an intolerable situation. You won't believe what I've walked into. Yes, I would rather be there working on briefs, thank you." Over her shoulder, she warned Quentin, "Five minutes, if you please. No longer."

"Yes. I'll hurry." Quentin began to push his way through the milling throng, headed for his bedroom. He could hear Billy saying something to him, but he ignored his roommate. He had no interest in anything the man had to say at this point. As it was he'd be in for a detailed lecture from Melissa on his permitting Billy to run wild, and the longer he took the hotter her temper would run.

She didn't display any emotions in public. In private was another story.

"Quinn, man, wait."

Quentin refused to slow down. He opened his bedroom door and, with no small degree of shock, found two students kissing on his bed. His mouth hung open in disbelief. "What the—what on God's green earth—"

"There you two are." Billy had appeared behind Quentin. "Look, partying after study group wraps up is one thing. You get up to this kind of shit, you'll be in for a world of hurt. Come on, out of Quinn's room. Out." The students scrambled up, laughing. "Not funny, kids. You want to go play smacky-mouth, do it somewhere else, on your own time."

Quentin stood frozen in shock. His sanctuary invaded. God. Had this happened before?

Billy touched him on the shoulder, causing Quentin to startle. "Hey, calm down. I'll talk to those two again. This was completely uncalled for."

"You really don't care about how much trouble you put yourself at risk for, do you?" Quentin felt oddly calm. "Smoking, drinking, letting your hair down..."

"Speaking of which, should I cut this or let it grow out longer? I kind of like longer." Billy tossed his red-tipped locks. "The color could stand a touch-up."

"I have absolutely zero time to discuss anything so trivial with you. If you don't mind, I'll be packing a bag. You won't have to deal with me tonight." Quentin moved into his room, reached under his bed for a duffle and placed it on top of the rumpled covers. "That should make you happy, at least."

"What are you talking about?" Billy lounged in Quentin's doorway, annoyingly refusing to go anywhere else. "Having you around doesn't make me unhappy. I like you, Quinn."

"That warms my heart. Now, if you don't mind leaving me alone?"

"Nah. I don't just like you, Quinn. I *like* you." Billy crushed his cigarette out in Quentin's potted fern and sauntered into the room. With his hands tucked into his pockets and his hips thrust forward, he was walking temptation.

Quentin tore his gaze away and focused on the bag he was filling with pajamas Melissa had bought him, a nice sweater and clean pair of trousers, socks...

"Don't look away from me. I saw that woman. *That* is the Melissa you've been sighing over every damn day since we met? She's like a Popsicle without the sweet flavoring. Ice on two stick legs. Come on, Quinn. A woman like her does it for you?"

"She's almost my fiancée," Quentin said firmly, although his lips felt numb. "Please don't speak ill of her in my presence."

"So I can say whatever I want as long as you're not listening? And you're definitely not listening to me." Billy turned and called out the doorway, "Hey, anyone else see the Ice Bitch who was just at the door? What a cunt, huh?"

"Billy!" Quentin zipped his bag with a vicious jerk. "I'll only warn you one more time."

Billy turned back. "And then what? You'll get violent? I'd like to see if you could take me down." He licked his lips, leaving them glistening in the low light of the lamp those students must have turned on. "Bet you could. You're thin but I've seen those muscles. How'd you like to have me on the ground underneath you, wrestling to see who comes out on top?"

"Billy, don't." Quentin picked up his case. "I have to go out and meet Melissa. We're going to a bed and breakfast for the night, and a taxi is waiting for us."

"Oh, so you can afford to treat her on your salary? She must be a sweet piece of ass to rate the swanky treatment." Billy came closer. "How come you and I never go anywhere nice?"

"We never go anywhere at all. Now, if you'd kindly move…"

"Why?" Billy stood firm, blocking the doorway. "Jesus, Quinn, open your eyes. You don't belong with someone like her."

"And who do I belong with? You?" Quentin blurted. His hand flew to his mouth, but too late. Billy's eyes had hooded, and his grin became predatory. "Billy, move out of the way."

"Don't think I will. You've actually considered it, haven't you?" Billy drew closer. Quentin could have darted around him and been out the door, but his feet felt stuck to the floor. Billy sauntered closer, gazing down into Quentin's eyes, making him feel like "Quinn" again. "You want to know what it's like being with me."

"I live with you."

"Not the same thing. You remember the times we've kissed, sugar? I do. You taste delicious, like mouthwash and toothpaste, all minty. You're so squeaky-clean that I'm dying to get you good and dirty." Billy's tongue flickered out again. "Ditch the woman. I'll kick my students out and we can spend the night getting to know each other better."

"I already know everything I want to about you. You're trying to... I don't think it's wise. And I'll be on my way now, if you don't mind." Finally able to move, spurred on by desperation, Quentin elbowed past Billy and headed for the door.

He stopped when a sharp whistle from behind him drew his attention. He turned slowly to see Billy digging in one pocket of his faded jeans. "Your loss. But hey, don't do anything I wouldn't do, and play it safe." He withdrew two foil packets and tossed the condoms to Quentin, who caught them on reflex. "When you get tired of someone who's just using you as a walking dildo, I'll be here. Maybe even tonight."

Quentin felt unbearably tired. He didn't even have the strength to muster up a response. All he could do was stare at Billy with utter weariness.

Billy ran a hand down his chest, fingers teasing at the button on his jeans. "I'll be thinking of you. Who are you going to be thinking of?"

Quentin's mouth opened, then closed. *Oh, God.*

Without a single look behind himself, he fled.

Chapter Seven

"Well. At last, a place with a little taste and some peace and quiet. Good choice, Quentin." Melissa took off Quentin's coat and folded it over her arm. "Where do we check in? I assume you know."

Quentin looked around himself in confusion. This wasn't the sort of bed-and-breakfast he had expected where there would be acres of chintz and lace with a kindly grandmother type behind a small counter, beaming and welcoming them inside her establishment. Instead, the place was done in gleaming chrome and glass, with no sign whatsoever of a reception area.

Someone had to have taken his call, though, when he made the reservations. Knowing it would make him look like a fool, and wincing at the thought of the inevitable repercussions, he cleared his throat and called, "Hello?"

Melissa made a noise of disapproval. "Quentin. You didn't even familiarize yourself with the location?"

"I'm sorry, Melissa."

She straightened the sharp collar of her blouse. "Perhaps you'd better call me Ms. Rife until we're in the rooms."

"Rooms?" Had she not heard him earlier, or paid attention when he'd specified a room for one and told her it had a queen-sized bed? "I...I only rented one, Melissa. Don't you remember my saying so?"

"Ms. Rife. Why would you only rent one? What sort of sleeping arrangements did you have in mind?" Melissa looked oddly discomfited. "Quentin, you really shouldn't assume things. I have studying to do, and I imagine you need to prepare course lectures."

Quentin shook his head. "It's a Friday night, Melissa." He felt a shot of anger. "Ms. Rife. Honestly, do I have to call you that? We're all but engaged."

"Verbal agreements are in place, but nothing is concrete until I have the ring you promised. Unless the ring is in your possession at this moment and about to appear on my finger, we're still only seeing one another. I won't chance any slurs on my reputation."

"That was your understanding of our arrangement?" Quentin was baffled and feeling a slow burn of—something— welling up inside of him. "I thought we'd discussed this."

"Yes, we did. However, things change, Quentin. Dr. Whiteside." Melissa took an impatient look around. "You should have done your research. What applies in academia applies in the real world. Ah-ha. You see?" She strode forward to a small bell sitting on a counter. One touch had a soft chime ringing. "A little deduction and we're all set, Professor."

A tall, thin woman with a slightly hooked nose appeared from a closed door off to one side. Her smile seemed a little tight and forced. Quentin had no idea how old she might be, but her skin bore the tell-tale signs of a facelift and other plastic surgeries. "Ah. Late-night arrivals. Whiteside and Rife? I had begun to give up on your putting in an appearance."

"Professor Whiteside had some things to take care of, hence the delay." Melissa seemed to have recognized either a worthy opponent or an ally. She took a firm stance and folded her arms over her chest, still holding Quentin's coat. "If you'll show us to our rooms?"

"One room," the woman corrected. "I don't have any other vacancies for the night."

"I only saw three cars out in the parking lot."

"Be that as it may, we're full. Do you think I'd turn down the chance at payment for a second room? You'll simply have to suffer through sharing accommodations for the night."

Melissa sighed. "At least the room will have two beds, correct?"

"Incorrect. The room has one queen-sized bed, as per Dr. Whiteside's request. There is a fairly comfortable couch, however, if one of you chooses to sleep there. Will you need an extra pillow and blankets?"

"No," Quentin said, just as Melissa decisively put in, "Yes."

The woman looked irritated. "Which will it be?"

Melissa glanced at Quentin, a stern look designed to put him in his place. "We'll take the extra bedding."

Quentin began to recognize the burning feeling inside his stomach. Fury. He tried to force it back down, but the stubborn sensation came back. Melissa wanted him to sleep on the couch of the room he'd splurged on for the both of them? He had no doubt that she'd appropriate the bed.

Hey, anyone else see the Ice Bitch who was just at the door? he heard Billy asking in his head. *What a cunt, huh?*

Quentin squashed his internal protest as Melissa finished dickering with their hostess about how many pillows, blankets and what the continental breakfast in the morning included. "I would prefer fruit and whole-grain toast," she said firmly. "So would Dr. Whiteside. No eggs, no bacon, nothing greasy or fatty."

Their hostess gave a thin smile. "I'll be sure to convey your instructions to the chef. Which would be myself. Now, if you'll follow me?"

"Dr. Whiteside, come." Melissa snapped her fingers. "Carry my luggage if you don't mind. Our room is upstairs and to the left." She held a key in her other hand. "We may as well take a look before we decide if this is good enough for our needs."

Snapping her fingers, as if I'm a dog that she's bringing to heel. The insult stung. Quentin picked up Melissa's suitcase and dress bag, managing to grab his own duffel, and followed in her wake. She smelled of a light, floral perfume that wafted back as he walked behind her, climbing a set of winding stairs. Despite his churning anger, Quentin inhaled and held on to the scent as long as he could.

It doesn't matter what she says or does, he told himself. *If I don't have Melissa in my life, I'll have no rock to cling to. If there's no Melissa, then that leaves me alone. Wide open. And then Billy... No.*

Quentin pulled up short as Melissa came to an abrupt stop. "This appears to be the room." She thrust her key into the lock and made a small noise of satisfaction as the door opened. "Come in, Dr. Whiteside. We'll take a look around."

He followed her inside, dropping the heavy suitcase as soon as he could. His fingers ached from the weight. Melissa must have brought her entire course load of texts with her. Was there anything in there besides books?

Melissa turned on a lamp and stood for a moment in an attitude of thoughtful consideration. She made various noises of approval or disdain, depending on what she glanced at. Her preferences made no sense to Quentin, who couldn't see anything that wasn't cold, steel or white. He felt more as if he were in a hospital room than a bed-and-breakfast.

"I suppose it'll do." Melissa rendered her judgment at last. She handed Quentin's coat to him. "Hang this up before it gets wrinkled. The closet is to your left. No, Quentin, your direct left. Honestly, do I have to do everything by myself? It's a wonder you got through graduate school." She snatched the coat back and pulled open a nearly invisible door flush with the wall. "Hang my dress bag. I'll be wearing that outfit on the ride back tomorrow."

Quentin obeyed. He took in a deep breath, finding his calm center, reminding himself of how much he needed her, how her strictness and stern direction kept him firmly in line, and then reached out for Melissa's hand. He squeezed her cold fingers and, when she didn't protest, pulled her into a careful hug. "It's wonderful to see you again," he said, and was relieved to find he meant it. "I'm glad you're pleased with the room."

"I didn't say pleased," was her arch answer as Melissa maneuvered herself out of Quentin's arms. "Put my suitcase in the corner, if you will? By the table. I'll need to access those books soon."

Quentin wavered between the books and the bed. "I'd hoped we could spend a little time together before you got down to studying."

"What else have we been doing?" Melissa tsked. "You've had plenty of opportunity to catch up on old times. I need to get this studying done. Amuse yourself around the room if you wish, but keep it down." She put her pocketbook on top of the tables, then pulled out her PDA and cell phone.

The phone clicked open first, her finger hitting speed-dial again. "Charles? Oh, I see. You're his wife. My apologies. Is Charles available? This is Melissa Rife. We're in several classes together. I need to confer with him over an issue that's arisen in part of our coursework. Yes, I'll wait. Thank you."

She glanced at Quentin. "Well, don't just stand there. Unpack your things."

Quentin hesitated. "You must know this Charles fairly well."

"He's my study partner," Melissa said shortly. "We've spent a considerable amount of time together. Don't tell me you're jealous, Quentin. Honestly. Unpack your things and then make up the couch."

"I'm not tired yet."

"I certainly am. You've been nothing but a source of stress ever since you called me to come and visit. I need for you to be quiet now, do you understand?" Melissa returned her attention to the phone. Quentin couldn't help but notice that her voice warmed up to something approximating human pleasure as she spoke. "Charles, yes. Your wife seems very nice. Of course I didn't say anything unwarranted by the situation. What do you take me for? Now, the McClark case. I think they could file a motion for injunction. What would be your opinion?"

As she talked away, Quentin tucked his tail between his legs and began to unpack. Melissa liked things just so. The dresser was easy enough to find. As he took out his meager change of clothing, refolded the articles and put them away, he fought down the anger that had risen back up and threatened to take him over.

Quentin didn't like the feeling. It reminded him too much of days gone by, when he'd been far too quick to speak and take action.

Slow, Quentin, slow. Take your time. Melissa's not going anywhere. Neither are you. Put the things away in their proper fashion, and hope she'll approve. Perhaps she'll consent to a little bit of romance in the evening.

The small Billy that seemed to have taken up residence inside Quentin's head snorted. *If she likes things arranged just so, why doesn't she do it herself? Fuck knows she's got everything else the way she wants it. Romance? Jesus, man, she made you call her Ms. Rife. And who's this Charles she's talking to? She's a hell of a lot nicer to him than she is to you. Better watch out, friend. I smell trouble.*

Quentin deliberately stopped thinking. It could only get him into hot water. With his clothes put away and his duffel neatly stowed, he made up the couch—which did not look comfortable in the least with its hard, flat pillows and chrome arms—then turned to the shining silver telephone. A discreet plate gave him a directory of numbers to call. Hoping it wasn't too late in the evening, he dialed the main line in the hopes of room service.

No answer.

"Melissa, would you excuse me for a moment?" Quentin waited for her reply, but got only an impatient wave of her hand as she chatted on to Charles. "Are you hungry? I could go and get us something to eat."

"Charles, excuse me." Melissa covered the phone with her hand. "Have you lost your senses? Food this late at night? You'd be lucky to find an open drive-through, and you know I don't eat fried foods at any time or take carbohydrates after seven p.m. You should have thought to bring a snack if you wanted to eat. Of course, I'm not going to stop you if you want to go and gorge yourself on whatever you please."

She turned her attention back to the conversation on her cell phone. Quentin hesitated. His stomach rumbled, as he'd skipped dinner to be sure he was at the train station early enough. There *was* a fast-food restaurant within walking distance. He could put on his coat, travel a couple of blocks and eat a relatively light meal. They had salads. Melissa would likely still be talking when he returned.

Fuck that, Quentin's internal Billy piped up. *You know she's only gonna bitch at you for eating this late at night. Now, if you were here with me, I'd fix you a double bacon cheeseburger and to hell with the calories. You'd work 'em off pretty soon. Nothing like sexercise.* Quentin could almost see Billy's eyebrows waggling. *Not that you're likely to get any tonight. How's that couch looking?*

Quentin sighed and sat on the edge of the bed. He rubbed his temples, hoping to stave off the incipient headache he felt building. Aspirin. Did Melissa have any?

Standing, he crossed to the table and touched his fiancée's shoulder lightly. She twitched irritably. "What now, Quentin?"

"Do you have any painkillers? I've got a bit of a—"

"All I have is Vicodin. You can't have any. They were prescribed for me. I don't carry anything else. Now, for the last time, stop interrupting my conversation. I can only continue to talk with Charles for a little while longer, and we need to cover these questions."

"And after you're done talking with Charles?" Quentin ventured.

"Then I'll study."

"I see." Quentin stood simmering for a moment. "So you're going to ignore the fact that I rented this room for a night with my fiancée, not ask why I wanted you to come up here, and deny me your company now that you are in town. Is that about it?"

Melissa's face darkened and her lips thinned. "Excuse me, Charles," she said tightly. "I have a personal situation to deal with. I'll call you tomorrow from the train and we'll finish this discussion then."

She clicked off her phone, tossed it down on the table and stood with her hands on her hips. "How dare you?" she spat. "I have business to conduct, Quentin. Haven't I told you not to interrupt me when I'm otherwise occupied?"

Quentin tried to hold back the words, but they refused to stop coming. "Melissa, you've been treating me as if I'm a stranger or, worse, a lech. You wouldn't even hold my hand. I had thought we were more than friends. And friends, at least, are known for a simple 'how are you doing' when they meet after an extended time apart."

"You're saying that I haven't treated you kindly? I came up here to see you, Quentin. That in itself should tell you that I've a vested interest in how you're doing. I've seen for myself that you've made a shambles of the life I helped construct for you. No interest in bettering yourself, sharing accommodations with a rapscallion smoker, failure to procure adequate lodging... You've disappointed me. What else do I need to know?" Melissa tapped her foot. She still hadn't taken off her heels. "Is there anything else you need to say?"

Quentin felt torn between a flood of angry words and the need to obey for the sake of trying to stay in Melissa's good graces. In the end, he swallowed his irritation and bowed his head. "No, Melissa."

"What did you expect, Quentin? I'd step off the train and we'd meet in slow-motion, arms open, with a violin playing in the background? You've always been far too much of a romantic. What we have is a business arrangement, not a case of hearts and flowers." She sniffed as if she smelled something bad. "What do you want, Quentin? A cozy tête-à-tête over hot cocoa, in which we'll share our deepest thoughts and come away all pink and fuzzy around the edges?"

Quentin bit back a hostile reply. "No, Melissa," he lied stiffly. "I wouldn't expect any such thing from you." And that, at least, was honest.

The fault was his own. He knew what Melissa was like. To expect warmth and compassion from her was like pleading for rain in the desert. Melissa didn't exude anything approaching the attitude of a confidante. She never had. But it hadn't mattered until now.

He'd been...content...to let her rule his life.

Melissa didn't seem willing to let this drop. "What do you want, Quentin?" she demanded. "Sex?" She heaved a sigh and sat on the bed. "If it'll calm you down, then fine. But just a quick one. I don't have time for anything protracted. Then again, you tend to finish quickly."

Quentin stood very still, the implied insult smarting, as Melissa slipped out of her suit coat. She folded it precisely across one arm of the couch. "Quentin, do hurry," she said, impatient. "You know what I like."

"Of course." Quentin's heart began to speed up. Surely a quick session in Melissa's arms would set his world back on course. He liked females, only females now, and this would reinforce his conviction. Glancing at Melissa's trim legs and slender arms, he concentrated on enjoying the sight. Hasty but careful, he slipped his sweater off over his head, laid it neatly aside and began to work on the buttons of his undershirt.

"Let's not take all night, Quentin," Melissa scolded. She shimmied out of her skirt and draped it across a cold white chair, revealing a set of sheer thigh-high hose and a pair of black satin panties.

Quentin's eyes were drawn directly between her legs. *The female genitalia,* he thought, pausing to appreciate the sight. Or try. *I'm assuming she'll want to be pleasured first.*

Which wouldn't be altogether a bad thing. His cock hung utterly limp within his trousers, one-hundred-percent unaffected by the sight of Melissa removing her clothes with businesslike efficiency.

She hesitated when she reached her shirt. "I'll just keep this on," was her decision. "My breasts are tender. I'm sure you don't understand, but there is such a thing as premenstrual syndrome and I'm not up to having any fiddling around with my nipples tonight." She sat on the bed, then lay down as if she were preparing for a doctor's exam. Utterly asexual and uninspiring. "Take off your pants and come join me. Don't be all night about it."

Quentin frowned. Normally, Melissa enjoyed manipulating her breasts while he attended to her female center. She'd complained of the same syndrome before, but never disapproved of his looking, at least. "Why?" he asked slowly, heart beginning to beat in the back of his throat. "Can I at least see you?"

Melissa's hand went to the securely fastened top button of her blouse. "I'd prefer that you didn't, Quentin."

She's hiding something from you, his internal Billy warned. *Get a look under that shirt. There's only one reason a woman doesn't want to show off her titties to her lover. What doesn't she want you to see?*

"Melissa, please remove your blouse." Quentin stood firm, his pants still on. "I'd like you to."

"And that's your reason for why I should remove more than I'm comfortable with?"

"At least undo some buttons. I'll feel like I'm making love to a nun."

Melissa snorted. "Making love? Quentin, choose your words with more care. This is merely sex. You appear to be in need of some release, and I'm choosing to permit you to take liberties with my body. We are, however, running out of time." She lay utterly still. "The offer is only on the table for a little while longer."

Quentin drew closer. Hesitantly, he reached down to run his hand along the length of her arm. Goose bumps followed in his wake. She wasn't entirely unresponsive, then.

Why he did what he did next, he would never know. Perhaps it was the way her lips automatically shaped a name, or the way she flinched. Whatever the reason, the result was the same. Quentin stared at the sheer white blouse covering Melissa's chest, and saw *it* underneath. Strawberry red and blossoming on the curve of one trim breast.

A love bite.

Quentin jerked back as if he'd been burned. "Who is Charles?" he asked through numb lips. "What is he to you?"

Melissa looked startled, then gave him a flat look. "What do you think? A woman has needs, Quentin. And, sadly, you're not around to satisfy those needs. But he's only a source of temporary relief." Her teeth were sharp and white as she smiled. "We, on the other hand, are all but engaged. Isn't that right?"

Quentin's throat closed up on whatever he might have said. Instead, silently, he turned and began to pack his things back in their duffel.

Melissa sat up, brisk as an automaton in every movement as she swung her legs off the bed. "Quentin, be rational."

Quentin continued to pack. His mind was racing and his mouth closed. He didn't trust himself to speak.

"Quentin, if you walk out that door right now, I don't expect to hear from you again. Are we clear? You and I will be finished if you leave me now. And then who will you have?"

Quentin coughed involuntarily, clearing his chest. "I don't know," he said quietly. "I don't know. Goodbye, Melissa."

ᏆᏟᏴᏚᎠ

Quentin unlocked the door to the faculty housing building in utter silence. He still had a lump in the back of his throat that wouldn't go away no matter how many times he swallowed. His duffel hung heavy in his hands, feeling as if it contained much more than a few articles of clothing.

The apartment was quiet and, for the most part, dark. The students had cleared out. Cups still dotted every available surface, their condensation making rings on all the furniture. Quentin could see a wet patch on his beloved recliner. Smoke hung thick and heavy in the air.

He couldn't bring himself to care.

Carefully shutting the door behind him, Quentin began to make his way toward his bedroom. He'd gotten halfway there when Billy appeared as if from nowhere, lounging against the frame of his bedroom door. He wore low-riding sleep pants in blue flannel and no shirt, the muscles in his chest both hard and rippling as he moved. "What, she didn't want you to sleep over?" The words were taunting, but the voice kind. Sympathetic. "So you didn't have a good time?"

Quentin hesitated, then shook his head. His fingers began to tremble.

"I didn't think you would." Billy reached for something just inside his door and came back with an unlit cigarette. He toyed thoughtfully with the white cylinder. "What happened?"

Quentin said nothing. His shoulders slumped a little as he quaked.

"Listen, man, it can't be that bad. She didn't kick you out, did she? Or did she? A lover's spat gone bad?" Billy began to grin. "So you came back here to your quiet little room. Too bad I'm here, right? But then again, that's me. Always in your way. You can't get rid of me, Quinn." Billy reached out with his free hand and laid it on Quentin's chest. "I'm inside there, whether you want me to be or not. You didn't come back because you had no place else to go. You came here for me."

Quentin's tremors became full-fledged shakes. His mouth went utterly dry. He swallowed hard, feeling himself half-choke. The duffel bag fell out of his nerveless fingers onto the floor.

Billy moved forward, dropping his cigarette. He cupped Quentin's chin in one hand. Bright blue eyes gazed into his own as he tipped Quentin's head up. "What did she do to you?" Billy asked softly.

It was one of the defining moments of his life. Voices screamed inside his head: *no, yes, no, yes, no, yes...* He was approaching a cliff, which once jumped off, he could never climb again.

God help him, though. He couldn't seem to stop himself.

He didn't want to turn away from this.

He wouldn't—couldn't—stop himself from being "Quinn" again.

Slowly, Quentin—no, Quinn—raised his hand to Billy's shoulder. He placed the other one on Billy's waist. The man's skin was warm and seemed to welcome Quinn's touch, as if Quinn were someone worth spending time on.

Shivering with emotions he couldn't put a name to, his cock starting to fill, Quinn leaned forward and pressed his mouth to Billy's, pleading with the man to accept, to understand and to forgive.

He hung there for what felt like forever before Billy's arms encircled him and pulled him close. "I thought so," Billy rumbled against Quinn's lips. "You figured out where you belonged. Right here. With me."

He kissed Quinn back, and time ceased to exist.

Chapter Eight

The short, narrow hallway was charged with an electricity that began at a low hum and kept building with every breath, every movement. Quinn clung to Billy, never wanting to let go. He knew he was probably hurting with the strength of his grip, but couldn't stop himself from hanging on. What was this? Solace for one night? A headlong dive into some space of time where he didn't have to think or worry? Or more?

The more Quinn wavered, the tighter he hung on.

"Hey. Hey, it's okay. Calm down." Billy withdrew from the kiss and began stroking Quinn's arms, running from shoulder to wrist with the lightest of touches. "It's not like I haven't wanted you from the moment we met, but this isn't a race. Chill."

Quinn buried his face in the curve of Billy's neck. A strange place to find himself in, but it felt like home. "No. I have to go ahead and do this. I need to..."

"Hush. Shh." Billy carefully took Quinn's hand in one of his own. "I'm getting the message." He laid the other hand lightly over Quinn's cock, the gentle pressure and heat of his palm sending Quinn into a new fit of shakes. "You finally realized what you wanted. Who you wanted. It's cool. There's time. We can take all night if you want."

Quinn leaned into Billy's solid warmth. His world was crumbling around him, and he needed an anchor. This man, the person who'd been driving him crazy for months, was something he could cling to, even though it meant fighting against everything that had been ingrained in his mind. But the denouncements were melting too quickly, like snow on a hot day. "Melissa...she's been cheating on me," he managed to say. "Someone named Charles. He's married. But you knew that, didn't you?"

"Not the details, not for sure. But I figured something was wrong. Hell, there couldn't be much right with a woman like her. God, Quinn. She's had you tied up in knots since you met, hasn't she? Wrapped you around her little finger and kept you there. That's why you've been so tense." Billy reached around and began to stroke Quinn's back. "C'mere. Inside my room, now."

Quinn struggled with himself. A part of him, deep inside, was screaming at him to run, run, run. Another part had come alive at the thought of going into Billy's private quarters.

Logic, he decided, had only caused him grief. It had frayed his nerves to the snapping point and won him a fiancée who didn't think twice about cheating.

To hell with it all, everything, his past and his future. He'd follow his emotions for one night. Just one night. Depending on what happened, he'd deal with things when and as he had to.

Billy would understand.

Quinn brought one hand up to caress Billy's cheek— asking, without words, for reassurance.

Billy leaned in to kiss Quinn again, brushing their lips together in no more than a passing touch. He tugged at Quinn's wrist. "Come on. Follow me. No more wasting time."

Quinn obeyed automatically. Step by step, he made his way into Billy's room. In a vague sort of way, he noticed the small details—several ashtrays overflowing with cigarette butts, ragged posters of screaming rockers on the walls, no lights on, and the mussed state of Billy's sheets.

Oh, God, his bed.

Despite the flutter of panic, Quinn continued to move forward. He was used to taking orders. All the same, his heart still pounded raggedly as he walked into the small room. This was it. He was really about to pass the true point of no return. He shuddered again, coming to a stop halfway in. *I can't do this. But I need...I need...*

"Quinn." Billy had stopped too. He turned back to Quinn and raised a hand to cup his jaw. "It's okay, man. I want you hard and fast. God damn, but I've dreamed about you in my bed. Still, it's okay that you need a little time. I can be patient."

Quinn laughed, a short bark of disbelief.

"There are hidden depths to me." Billy grinned in his infectious, charming way. For the first time since they'd met, Quinn smiled back tremulously. "See? You're better already. C'mon. Promise I won't do anything until I get the all clear."

Billy led Quinn forward. Quinn went without much external hesitation. Inside his mind, his thoughts were flapping around like a butterfly trapped in a bottle. *It's wrong. It's wrong. It's wrong.*

God. Why does it feel so right?

What happens after we do this? Later tonight? Tomorrow?

I don't really know what I'm doing, do I? But here I go...

"You're thinking too hard. Makes my own brain hurt." Billy reached the edge of his bed, broader and longer than Quinn's, and eased Quinn down to a sitting position. "Scoot on in. Next to the wall."

"My shoes?" was all Quinn could think to say.

"Yeah, messy. We can take those off." Billy knelt and, with gentle hands, began to undo the laces of Quinn's sneakers. "New, huh? Bet you wanted to impress Melissa with how sparkly white they are. But nothing impresses her, does it?"

Quinn shook his head mutely. "Probably should have worn dress shoes. She likes—liked things formal."

Billy snorted, the sound worth a thousand words. He slid one sneaker off, and then the other, his hands nimble and light. He stroked Quinn's sock feet, starting at the ankle and moving down to the arch. The sensation tickled, yet it sent a bolt of desire through Quinn. When was the last time someone had touched him as if they cared how he felt?

He couldn't remember.

"Go on, lie down," Billy urged. "Get comfortable. Neither of us is going anywhere. Unless you mind the smoke?"

The air was thick, redolent with the remains of cigarette fumes, but Quinn didn't mind. The place smelled like Billy. He slowly lowered himself onto his side, then scooted back until his shoulders touched the wall.

Watching, he took in the sight of Billy carefully easing into place just opposite himself. As Billy leaned his head against the pillow, the dim light from outside struck the red tips of his hair and made them gleam.

Billy grinned, his face a half-mask in the shadows, but oddly reassuring. "See? We're in the same bed and you haven't been struck down by lightning yet."

"It's—it's wrong," Quinn managed, not sure why he was protesting.

"Yeah? Says who? Some people who messed with your head?"

"How—how did you know?"

"Educated guess. They were the ones who were wrong, Quinn. It's okay, I swear. Something that feels so damn good can't be bad. It's lying to yourself that's wrong." Billy began to touch Quinn again, light and gentle as a man could, running his hands over Quinn's chest. "Come here."

Quinn shifted closer, uncertain as to what he should do.

"Yeah, it's been a while, huh? Look. Lift your head and let me get my arm under there. You can rest on my shoulder." As Quinn moved into position, Billy pressed a hard kiss to the top of Quinn's head. "Just lie still for a minute. Take some deep breaths. Swear to God I'm not going to hurt you."

Quinn licked his suddenly dry lips and swallowed around a knot in his throat. "Do you promise?"

"Cross my heart." Billy began to rock Quinn, a lazy movement, like he could take all night doing nothing else. Holding Quinn as if he understood. *Really* understood. "Trust me, man. Have some faith."

"I can feel you," Quinn whispered. "You're hard."

Billy chuckled. "Yeah. You kind of have that effect on me. The first time I saw you, I got hard. You know, I suspected you were gay and repressing—there's a vibe, right? Figured I wasn't going to get anywhere with you, though, at least not at first. But guess what? I kept on waiting. It's been a couple of months. I can keep it in my pants until you stop shaking."

"I'm sorry. I don't mean to." *Shaking. God, I'm still trembling like a heroine with the vapors. When will this settle down? I've jumped in with both feet. I shouldn't be afraid of falling anymore.*

"Shut it." Billy kissed Quinn's forehead. "No apologies. Nothing until you're ready for it. Just let me be here for you." He continued rocking Quinn, each slow to-and-fro motion soothing his jangled nerves.

"Thank you," Quinn breathed. He would have gone on to thank Billy for everything he was doing, but got the feeling Billy understood without his having to say the words.

Softly, Billy began to sing. Some quiet tune that should have had a slow, sweet guitar accompanying it.

Quinn let out a long breath as he recognized the song. "'Because the Night'. I heard Natalie Merchant sing it once on *Unplugged*. I used to like her back then."

"Oh, yeah. Damn good lyrics." Billy went on singing about desire, hunger and feasts of love. He stayed on key, half-singing and half-humming, each note thrumming into Quinn's bones. Impulsively, Quinn began to accompany Billy, his breath coming in quick jerks yet still managing to keep the tune.

Billy chuckled. "You know the words, I bet. 'Take my hand, and you'll understand.'"

Quinn reached for Billy's hand and clasped it. The man's skin was warm and dry, his palm broad and solid. He hung on as Billy said in his husky, cigarette voice, "They can't hurt you now. You know that, right?"

"The night belongs to lovers," Quinn whispered. "Does the night belong to us?"

"Damn right." Billy pressed his lips to Quinn's. Quinn felt Billy's tongue flicker out, not insistently, but as if to see if he were ready. Quinn gave one last tremor, then cautiously opened his mouth. The small groan Billy gave as he slid his tongue inside Quinn's mouth sent shock waves of desire through Quinn's body, bringing back all the old memories and a tide of pleasure.

115

Quinn surrendered himself to the kiss. Billy was gentle, stroking his tongue against Quinn's, not demanding anything that Quinn wasn't willing to give—but Quinn remembered how to do this. He twined his own tongue around Billy's, tugging slightly. The small, surprised noise Billy gave almost made Quinn laugh.

God, how long had it been since he'd been amused in bed?

Slowly, Quinn worked his hand down between their bodies. He ran his fingers across the hard planes of Billy's stomach, and then tugged at the waistband of the man's sleep pants.

"Stop." Billy pulled away from the kiss. "Jesus, Quinn." He gave a ragged breath. "I'm trying to give you time here, man."

Quinn shook his head. "I don't need time. I need you. Like water, like breath, like rain. LeAnn Rimes."

"Turning the songs around on me, huh? Who knew you were a country fan?" Billy moved closer to Quinn, his warmth at once frightening and so very welcome. "There's a lot about you I don't know. But you're going to give me the chance to find out."

Quinn nodded slowly. "Tonight," he said, not trusting himself to anything more. "Tonight."

Billy kissed him again, long, lingering and sweet, but growing hungry. "God, you taste good. Go on and touch me. I know you want to. I don't bite. Not unless someone asks me to."

Quinn took a deep breath. He pulled at Billy's waistband, but instead of dipping his hand inside, he laid it on the outside, feeling the man's cock hard and ready through his pants. The sensation almost made him dizzy. It'd been so long since he'd felt another dick in his palm, a steely column that he knew would have silk-soft skin and a core of pure iron. Billy inhaled appreciatively as Quinn cupped his cock, squeezing gently.

"Oh, yeah. Yeah. Keep on doing what you're doing. No, wait." He raised his hips and shimmied out of his sleep pants, pushing them down his thighs. "Now. Touch me."

Quinn licked his lips. He reached for Billy's cock again, feeling a small hitch in his chest as he cupped the hardness of the man's erection. His fingers began to travel, walking up the length, tracing thick veins. Billy was so beautiful naked, all his muscles set off by the dim glow of the lights.

How odd that the man should be wholly nude while he himself remained fully dressed. At first glance Quinn would appear to have the advantage, but he knew how well the tables were turned.

When Quinn reached the top of Billy's prick, he found it to be slightly wet and sticky. Semen. No, come. Pre-come. "Is this for me?" he surprised himself by asking.

"This, and a dozen wet dreams' worth." Billy chuckled. "You're doing great, Quinn. Keep going. Work me rougher."

Quinn wrapped his hand around the breadth of Billy's cock and squeezed. His eyes shut even tighter at the feel of the organ pulsing in his palm, so hard and alive, a separate being. He'd missed this, he realized, more than he'd known. More than he'd thought was possible. "So good," he whispered. "You feel like..."

"Heaven, huh? But not too much more of that, or this'll be over before it starts. No way it ends so fast. I've been dreaming about you for too long." Billy pushed Quinn away. "Your hand is about to drive me crazy, you know that? So, stop before I come. I want to make sure you have a good time. Turn over and lie on your back."

Quinn gave a ragged sigh and reluctantly let go of Billy's cock. Obedient, he rolled over and lay facing the ceiling.

Billy's face came into view. He pressed his lips against Quinn's, and Quinn's eyelids fluttered shut. "Keep them closed," Billy directed. "Don't look at anything. Just feel."

Quinn did as he was told. What he felt, though, drew a vivid mental map. Billy kissed a trail down his chest, each touch of his lips burning like a brand even through his shirt. When he reached the waistband of Quinn's trousers, Billy pulled the shirt out and nuzzled into the small arrow of hair leading down into his pants. "You smell good," he whispered hoarsely.

Quinn whimpered.

He felt Billy's hand resting on the button fastening of his pants. "I'm going to touch your cock. Stop me if you don't want this. *Really* don't want this. 'Cause once I start—no going back."

Shivering a little, Quinn nodded. He felt another kiss to his lower belly. "Knew you could," Billy murmured. He undid the pants slowly, one button at a time. Quinn jerked, the touch bringing back a whole new flood of memories. This time, though, he didn't try to push them away.

His cock came free of the pants, helped along by Billy's hand shoving them down. Quinn inhaled sharply. The cool night air burned against his overheated flesh. He thrust instinctively into Billy's palm, aching for the feel of a solid hand closing around his prick. *Just like old times.*

Older days than the ones with Melissa in them. Melissa had never... She didn't like to.

Billy loved it. Quinn could tell. "Fuck, but you're gorgeous. Hey, your eyes are still closed. Open up. I want you to watch me while I do this." He squeezed Quinn's cock. "Want to see your face light up."

As Quinn obeyed, Billy raised up to kiss him again, lingering, slipping his tongue in and out as he tightened and loosened his fist. "What do you think? This feel good?"

Nodding, Quinn made bold enough to reach up for another taste of Billy's lips. He was delicious, salty and ashy-bitter. "Do I taste like mint?" he asked abruptly.

Billy laughed. "Nah. Tears. Not all bad ones, though, huh? Don't jump, now. I'm gonna put my mouth somewhere else." His hand gripped hard around Quinn's cock. "Want to see what this tastes like."

"Oh, God. Yes. God, yes." Quinn reached up to touch Billy's cheek and thread his hand through the man's hair. "Please." His heart pounded. "I want you to."

"Hell, yeah." Billy shook himself loose and made his way back down to Quinn's cock. Quinn felt the hand surrounding his prick ease up a bit, but only to get a better grip. Billy pressed his lips to the tip of Quinn's dick, opened his mouth and—*oh, God.*

Heat suffused Quinn, filling him up as if he had a fever. Quinn's head spun as he felt the burning warmth of Billy's lips and mouth slowly devouring his cock. He gasped and grasped at the covers, searching for something to hang onto. Billy's free hand nudged his own. Their fingers tangled together.

Billy began to suck. Quinn drew in a sharp breath and stopped himself from bucking up. Instead, he lay there trembling as he felt the pressure of the man's mouth sliding up and down his length, no teeth at all, just hard sucking. Billy could take almost all of him, and he used his hand to cover the rest, point and counterpoint.

Almost too much, but at the same time not enough. Quinn made a small, needy sound.

Willa Okati

Billy was good with the cues. He began to use his tongue. Quinn groaned, gripping Billy's hand hard. Probably too hard, but he couldn't find it in himself to care. Billy squeezed back as if encouraging him. Letting himself go a little more, Quinn hung on for dear life as Billy licked and flicked and sucked, lavishing attention on Quinn's cock as if it were the best he'd ever tasted.

After a minute of hot action, Billy drew off long enough to blow several light, cool breaths over the iron heat of Quinn's cock. "Salty," he whispered. "Sweet. Love this. Can't wait for you to be ready to do this. Bet you forgot how good it is."

Quinn startled. "How—how did you know—"

"That sixth sense again. Easy now. Gonna make you see stars." Billy slid his mouth down over Quinn's cock again, applying pressure and suction at the same time. He carefully untwined his fingers from Quinn's and brought his other hand into play, rolling Quinn's balls and squeezing them with a light and easy touch.

Long practice, Quinn thought with an internal giggle. *He's so good at this. He's right, I'd forgotten—oh, God. God.*

He let out a ragged exclamation without words. Billy released Quinn's balls to begin kneading at his hip. Telling him it was all right. He could come, and it would be okay. Quinn didn't want this to end, God help him, but the orgasm was building up inside of him.

Billy's cheeks hollowed out as he sucked hard, and Quinn couldn't hold back any longer. He exploded inside Billy's mouth, feeling himself shoot hard and fast. Billy began to swallow, drinking the come down as quickly as it spurted in, his tongue bathing Quinn's cock as if he could milk some more out.

When the climax had finished twisting his insides, Quinn lay panting roughly, his vision fuzzing out at the edges. Billy drew off, kissing the tip of Quinn's cock, then coming back up

120

for a kiss. Quinn could taste himself as an added flavor in Billy's mouth. God, it had been so long, but he recognized the tang of semen. Musky, pungent, salty.

He kissed Billy back, not wanting to let him go.

Billy pulled away after a few moments of them sweeping each other's mouths. "There," he said, his voice low and satisfied as a cat in the cream. "You feel good, don't you? Told you it was all right."

Quinn laughed, the sound choppy through his ragged breathing. "I'm surprised," he managed to say. "I would have thought you'd be the one asking for a blow job."

"Why?"

"I came to you. Shouldn't I have been the one to give?"

"As you give, so shall you receive."

"And I thought you were always on top."

"Usually, I am. But this was a gift for you, Quinn. My way of saying welcome to the neighborhood." Billy's eyes sparkled. "'Course, if you want to return the favor, I'm not going to complain."

Quinn felt dizzy at the thought, but no...there was something he wanted more. "Billy?"

"Yeah?" Billy petted Quinn's hair. "You did so good, by the way. You were delicious. Not to mention the way you move. You could drive a man nuts even if he weren't already crazy for you."

"I want... I want..." Quinn took a steadying breath. He felt so exposed in nothing but a button-down shirt with only his sleeves loosened...yet it didn't feel like a bad thing. Especially when he could look over and see the expanse of Billy's naked body, hard and ready for what he wanted. "Fuck me," Quinn whispered. The words were unfamiliar after so long, but he pushed them past the last of his barriers and over his thick tongue. "I want to feel you inside me."

Something flared in Billy's gaze. Something hot and needy. "You're ready for that?" he asked, voice husky. "You sure?"

Quinn nodded. He reached down to Billy's cock and ran his fingers along the length. "I want this," he said. "So much. I was too afraid."

"And you're not, now?"

"No." Quinn willed away his lingering doubts. "Just...go easy, please? It's been years."

"Go easy. Man, I'll treat you like a prince." Billy bent his head, capturing Quinn's tongue with his own. "I've wanted to do this for so long. You on your back. Wide open. Me between your knees, fucking you hard as I can. Oh, yeah." He moved to lick Quinn's ear, tracing a path down from shell to lobe. The feeling tickled, tingled and sent a new shock of desire into Quinn's balls. "You want this bad, don't you? Say it."

Quinn nodded, realizing he was only being honest. He'd taken a step off the bridge, and now he was plummeting down into the deep waters with a gleeful scream. "I want this," he insisted. "Fuck me, Billy. Please."

"Your wish." Billy sat up. Quinn reached out to stroke him, his hand touching Billy's bare cock. Long, thick and dark with blood, it bobbed up to slap against Billy's hard stomach. Billy ran his fingers down the length, showing it off. "Take a good long look. This is gonna be inside you."

Quinn's mouth went dry with anticipation. "Yes. Please. Hurry?"

Billy let out a half-growl, half-laugh. "There's some supplies under your pillow. Lube and condoms. I've always been careful, but don't ever trust anyone who says that, hear?"

While part of Quinn's brain acknowledged the wisdom behind Billy's words, the rest of his mind was otherwise occupied. All that skin, Quinn thought, reacted, and reached out to touch. His fingers danced down Billy's cock, marveling at the strength and resiliency of the organ. "I trust you."

"Don't be stupid."

"No." Quinn shook his head. "More than condoms. You...you won't hurt me."

"Not if I can help it. Not like the others." Billy's face hardened for a moment before he shook his head and the grin returned. "Bet you still remember the moves."

"It's been a while."

"Doesn't matter. This is just like riding a bike."

"No training wheels?"

"Baby, you don't need them." Billy reached down to cup his cock, his stomach muscles rippling as he moved. The sight set Quinn's heart to racing again. "Want to feel you put the condom on. Need to have your hands on me."

Quinn raced to do as he'd been told. While the silky feel of Billy's cock in his hands was a carnal pleasure that made his heart race, in a small place in the back of his mind, he was still afraid. That fear, though, was being drowned by the pure *need* to touch and be touched, to find comfort in Billy's arms, to feel him pushing deep inside. He wanted to spread his legs wide for the man to come and fuck him. If that made him a slut, then he was a slut. He'd be the slut he had once been, and do it gladly.

"Please," he whispered as he finished smoothing the condom onto Billy's cock. "Inside me."

"Almost there," Billy soothed, reaching for the tube of lubricant and smoothing it on his sheathed cock. He squirted more into his palm. "Move for me, Quinn. Yeah, just like that.

Open wide. Spread those legs. Let me between your knees. Just like I dreamed. Raise up—oh, baby, yeah, you remember how."

Quinn closed his eyes as he felt Billy's fingers probing his hole. He was tight enough for this to hurt, but he didn't care. Billy was taking care of him. "Oh!"

"Man, you are tight. One finger."

Quinn felt the digit moving inside him and couldn't help but moan with pleasure.

"You want another?" Billy asked huskily.

Quinn struggled for control while caught in the middle of so much delight. "Yes," he said after a pause. He could do this. "Two."

"Yell at me if I hurt you." Billy withdrew, then pushed in with two fingers. Quinn gasped. The intrusion burned, but he remembered the pain as a prequel to something so good. The feel of this small part of Billy inside him made him want to spread wider, to thrust down and get Billy deeper.

Billy's fingers moved inside Quinn. "Found it," Billy said triumphantly, and pressed down on Quinn's prostate. Quinn almost came off the bed, his back arching up. "You like that. Knew you would."

"More," Quinn begged, his hand fisting in the covers. "Do it again. Please."

"You talk so pretty." Billy started up a slow massage, butting his fingers against the small lump deep within Quinn's hole. He stroked and rubbed, each thrust driving Quinn just a little further out of his mind.

Quinn could barely think. When Billy added a third finger and began to scissor them apart, stretching him open, he let out a ragged scream of pleasure/pain. It hurt so much, but felt incredible. Good. God, so good. He began to writhe, desperate for more. With a jolt, he remembered how to relax and let his body open.

"That's right. That's the way." Billy began thrusting his fingers in and out of Quinn's ass. "This is nothing. Wait till you feel my cock."

Oh, yes. God, yes. "Please," Quinn said, voice shaking again. "Now. No waiting."

Billy hesitated briefly and then acknowledged Quinn's readiness. "Okay. Hang on." He withdrew his fingers, wiping the wet and sticky lube off on his tangled blue sheet. Even though his hand was still a little slick, he used it to bring one of Quinn's legs up over his shoulder. He rubbed a slippery line down Quinn's calf. "Okay?"

Quinn managed to nod.

"Okay." Billy lifted the other leg, balancing Quinn so that his ass was raised and fully exposed. He moved forward, and Quinn felt the pressure of Billy's cockhead at his hole. "Now?"

Quinn nodded again.

Billy pushed. There was a brief moment in which the pain flared bright and hot, but then the head of his cock popped in and the searing heat faded to a glowing burn. A good pain. One Quinn had missed. He moaned, unable to speak, but wanting more.

Good thing Billy seemed able to read his mind—or just couldn't wait any longer. He worked his way into Quinn, one inch at a time, letting out small grunts and hisses of pleasure, not stopping until his balls slapped against Quinn's ass.

Holding them there, he asked, "Good?"

Quinn bobbed his head eagerly even as his eyes rolled back in his skull. It'd been so long since he'd been fucked. His body was going to burst with the bliss. *Doesn't matter if it's wrong. I'll deal with things later. Right now, I want to be fucked.*

"Gonna move," Billy warned. He withdrew in a slithery pull and then shoved back forward. Quinn yelled, but not from pain. He wanted this to go on forever.

Billy appeared to want the same thing. He thrust slowly in and out, each push building the pleasure spiral by spiral. The white-hot ecstasy made Quinn's own cock start to fill again, jerking up until it lay flat against his belly. "So hot," Billy rumbled. "Touch yourself."

Quinn didn't think his fingers could be that coordinated, but after a moment's fumbling while Billy held still, he managed to grasp his dick. "Jerk it," Billy ordered. "Hard. While I fuck you. Now."

He pushed in and out, still slow at first, waiting for Quinn to find the rhythm. When Quinn's hand was sliding up and down, his grip tight, drops of pre-come lubricating his fingers, Billy let out a noise of satisfaction and began to thrust hard, no holds barred.

Billy didn't do anything by halves. The force of his fucking shoved Quinn backward an inch at a time, until his head was banging on the scarred wooden headboard on the bed. He could hear the ancient bedsprings they lay on screaming in protest, and someone moaning as if they were a cat in heat.

He realized that he was the one making the noise. *So good, so hot, so fast. More, more, more...*

Billy held onto Quinn's legs with a death grip and thrust, his cock dragging over Quinn's sweet spot, plunging home with each stroke. "Good," he panted. "Fuck, yeah. Good."

Quinn couldn't answer. He was too caught up hanging on to the headboard to keep himself from battering his skull; too busy feeling the bolts of pleasure running through his own cock and the bliss of Billy's prick in his ass. He was stuffed to bursting with Billy's monster inside him, ready to explode—*oh!* Quinn let out a long, low wail as his orgasm hit, come streaming over his fingers and dripping onto his belly. The spasms squeezed all the muscles in his body and clamped down on Billy's cock.

"Fuck!" Billy swore, thrust one more time, ground down and came. Quinn could tell by the way he quaked. No come spurting into his ass due to the condom, but almost as good. He squeezed again, bearing down hard, working Billy's cock as if it were his own hand grasping the organ.

After a long moment, Billy shook his head. "Fuck," he repeated himself, his voice sounding exhausted, but in a good way. Slowly, he began to pull out. Quinn protested with a low sound, to which Billy laughed wearily. "More later," he promised. "You just about killed me. Gotta rest."

Without the connection of cock in ass, Quinn felt unbearably empty. He lay still, sore and aching but wanting to go again right away. Beads of sweat ran down his skin, mixing with the come on his belly and running off into the sheets. "Billy..." he pleaded as the man dealt with his condom, not knowing what he was asking for.

"Shh, shh." Billy lowered Quinn's legs and kissed one thigh. "Hang on a second." He eased himself off the bed and stumbled out into the hall. Quinn heard water running, and then Billy came back in with a wet hand towel. Rough, but not too hard, Billy sponged off Quinn's stomach and cleaned the lube from his ass. Then throwing the towel onto the floor, Billy lay back down beside Quinn, on his side, and dragged Quinn into a tight embrace.

"Yeah," he murmured into Quinn's hair. "Worth the wait. You're a prize." The edges of his red-tipped locks tickled Quinn's face. When Quinn glanced up at them, they shone like rubies.

Quinn let his eyes shut one more time in pleasure. He'd deal with all the fallout tomorrow. He'd already done this, so he would enjoy the afterglow. It'd been years since someone had held him after pounding his ass into the mattress.

Felt so good. Felt like the bad old times were suddenly all right again.

He yawned. *I'll figure it all out tomorrow. Right now, I need to sleep...*

"Rest," Billy said, running his fingers down Quinn's side. "I got you. Not going anywhere."

Quinn nodded dozily. He felt himself slipping away into the arms of Morpheus as Billy held him close. Warmth and the feel of a heart beating lulled him into slumber, where there were no more questions but just dreams of being in the arms of someone who cared enough to hold him, even if only for a while.

It was the best sleep he had experienced in far, far too long.

Chapter Nine

Quinn woke with the odd sense of being where he wasn't supposed to be. He squinted against the too-bright light of the sun dawning through an open window and unshuttered blinds, raised his hand to shield himself from the light...and remembered that his bedroom faced west.

Where then, was he?

Oh, God.

His mouth went dry as memories came rushing in. Melissa and her betrayal. Stumbling back home as a broken man, his head a jumbled mess. Falling into Billy's arms. The way Billy had held him, comforted him...slept with him...

Quinn shut his eyes tightly, his face contorting into a grimace. Voices began to assault him from every corner of his memory. Guardians. Counselors. Others. *How could you, Quentin? We taught you better. Man shall not lie with man. Transgression. Sin. Damnation.*

He heard Melissa, next. *Quentin, really, this is beyond the pale. You overreacted again and turned into a sniveling mess. What depths won't you sink to? Sleeping with that—that—man. If I'd known you would do something so foolish, I'd have locked the room door and not let you go.*

Her voice rang so strongly in his mind that Quinn almost expected to open his eyes, look up and see Melissa standing there dressed in her neat suit, one heel tapping on the messy floor of Billy's room. She'd rake her eyes critically over his naked body, barely concealed by a thin blue sheet, and give a minute shake of her head. Her chin would thrust out. *Quentin, get up and come with me. Don't make me wait. We're getting you back in therapy. I may, possibly, forgive you someday when you've earned it.*

Right. And until then, she'd sleep with Charles, because "a woman has needs". Quinn took in a deep breath and fisted the sheet tightly. He'd told himself he would think about these things "tomorrow". Well, the day had arrived, and he didn't know any more than the night before where he stood on the matter at hand.

All he knew was that he'd lain all night in the arms of someone who cared enough to comfort him when he was sick at heart. Someone who'd given him what he—to be honest with himself—had craved ever since trying to turn his life onto a straighter path. A plain-speaking, honest-dealing person who hadn't promised anything or offered any threats.

It might still be a bad idea, but Quinn couldn't help wanting this fragile bubble of contentment to last. Unclenching his hands, he took several deep breaths before deliberately banishing the scolding voices from his mind. To hell with them all, at least for the time being. This might be insanity, but reality was far too cold to face just then.

Billy. He needed Billy. Where was he?

Quinn reached out to run his hand across the space where Billy had lain. Still warm. He must not have gotten up too much earlier than Quinn himself. How odd that such a night owl should also be a morning person.

But he might have stayed until Quinn woke, mightn't he? Or had Billy stirred in his sleep, discovered who he lay with and fled in disgust?

Please, God, no. Quinn sat up, acutely aware of the ache in his ass and his total nudity. He swung his legs over the edge of the bed and grasped automatically for his pants, lying in a puddle on the floor, then hesitated. He had a hypothesis about how the morning was going, yes, but no way to test it.

Or did he?

Water was running in the bathroom. The shower, it sounded like, going at full blast. The air was growing moist, as if Billy had left the door open like he usually did. Warm and damp. Quinn could hear Billy singing over the sound of the water falling, some growly rocker tune Quinn didn't know.

Billy wouldn't be singing if he were in a bad mood, would he? And if he were anything like Quinn's past lovers, he would have kicked Quinn out of his bed the moment he woke up, not left him lying there.

Developing that hypothesis, Quinn slipped out of bed. It felt uncomfortable to be naked instead of garbed in pajamas or robe, but he deliberately shook off the feeling of discomfiture. His clothes lay on the floor in the midst of a tangle of empty cans, an overflowing ashtray and Billy's scattered wardrobe, but he left his own trousers and shirt alone. With one toe, he prodded at the flannel sleep pants Billy had been wearing. They were as soft and as rich a blue as he remembered, as deep a gentian shade as violets, if washed so often that they were faded at the knees.

Time to see how brave he could be. Trusting in the validity of his suspicions, Quinn made his way out of Billy's bedroom without getting dressed. The bathroom was directly across their narrow hallway, and, as he had predicted, the door was open a crack. Billy's singing was even louder out here, his rough voice ripping through the tune with gleeful abandon.

Quinn swallowed, feeling a lump go down his throat and settle heavily in his stomach. Fisting both of his hands, he raised one to knock on the door. "Billy?"

The singing went on.

Quinn tried again, sticking his head inside the door. A blast of steam hit him in the face, along with the rich smell of woodsy soap and fresh water. He raised his voice. "Billy? Are you in here?" A fool's question, but he couldn't think of anything else to say. "It's Quinn," he added, just in case Billy had forgotten.

There was a pause, then Billy pulled the curtain back. Water splattered on the floor, completely disregarded. The red streaks in his hair had gone a dark magenta when soaked. Beads of steaming water ran down his body, from nipples to impressive cock. The dark blond of his undyed hair matched the nest of curls at his groin.

Billy grinned broadly. "Hey, you woke up. I was gonna bring you breakfast in bed after I washed off."

Quinn felt unusually touched. No one had ever done something like that for him. And if Billy had planned to feed Quinn, then perhaps he wasn't regretting what they'd done the night before. "You were?"

"Yeah. I know you usually like all that health-food shit, but I was going to fix you eggs and bacon. Maybe a piece of fruit on the side." Billy's eyes twinkled. "So, you gonna come on in here, or do I have to come out and get you? You look good enough to eat standing there with everything swinging in the wind. C'mon, there's room for two."

Quinn blushed, but he stepped forward as he'd been bid. Billy held the shower curtain patiently until Quinn had carefully gotten in with him, then jerked it back. Before Quinn could adjust to the idea of being in a shower with another man after years without the treat, Billy seized him by the waist and ran one soap-slippery hand up his back. He pulled Quinn close and kissed him roughly, sliding his tongue into Quinn's mouth.

Quinn surrendered willingly. The feeling of being kissed as if he were desired was a heady one, flooding him with all sorts of endorphins, making him feel reckless. He brought his own hands into play, reaching down to squeeze Billy's ass cheeks.

Billy jumped a little and let out a laugh. Parting their lips, he chuckled and said, "Hey, you don't mess around, do you? Knew you wouldn't, though. Once you climbed out of your shell, no going back, right?"

Quinn wasn't too sure, but he nodded all the same. "Kiss me again?" The longer he and Billy were tangled together like this, the less he had to think. "More. Deeper. Harder."

"Fuck, yeah," Billy growled, bringing their mouths together a second time. He slanted his lips over Quinn's, nuzzling in for a hard kiss full of tongue and teeth, the embrace setting Quinn's head to spinning. His hands wandered over Quinn's back, leaving trails of fire in their wake until he reached Quinn's own ass. The feel of hands there made Quinn jump, but Billy gave them a playful squeeze all the same.

Billy sucked on Quinn's lip, then pulled off. This close, Quinn could really and truly see his eyes twinkling. "Good morning," he said softly, kneading Quinn's ass. "Some kind of way to wake up, huh?"

Quinn licked his lips. "Good morning," he answered, feeling suddenly shy and gawky and awkward. Billy was so practiced and polished at this that Quinn felt like a bumbling teenager again. He had to redeem himself somehow. "Do you want me to wash your back?" he blurted.

Billy cocked his head to the side, considering the question. "If you want to, sure. There's a washcloth hanging off the faucet."

"I know. You always leave one there, soaking wet." Quinn surprised himself by laughing. "And I always—"

"Yell at me about it, yeah. I know." Billy's fingers began to wander toward the crease of Quinn's ass. "You sore?"

Quinn shook his head. "Not too badly."

"Damn. I was hoping you'd remember me every time you sat down today."

"Rest assured, I will."

"You still have that Saturday class?"

"We have time." Quinn dared to raise his hand to stroke a line down Billy's wet spine. The water spattered off Billy's back. He himself was still mostly dry, feeling sandpapery, but he found that he didn't mind. A hunger was growing inside him. An inclination he hadn't given in to for...he couldn't remember how long. He cleared his throat. "I think I know something you'd like better than washing, though."

"Oh, yeah?" Billy's grin broadened a little. "What's going on in that head of yours, Quinn? New game?"

"New to me," Quinn answered honestly. "Or, at least, it's been a long, long time since I played."

"Will I like this game?"

"If I do it right." Quinn brought his hand around to press the palm against Billy's chest, mirroring his action of the night before. He could feel Billy's heart beating against his fingers, the pulse growing quicker. "Be patient with me?"

"Always. Go on and do what you want."

Quinn took in a deep breath. "All right. But no laughing at me. Do you promise?"

"Swear." Billy pressed Quinn's ass hard enough that he brought their groins into contact. Quinn realized that Billy was more than half-hard, and recognized the tingling in his own balls as the signal of a growing erection. "Mmm. This is good right here, though."

It would have been heaven just to stand there and let Billy lead him in rubbing off against one another, but now Quinn ached to act on his previous impulse. "No," he said. "Wait. I want to do this."

Billy pretended to pout. "Okay, do what you want. But the offer stands." He offered a lewd grin and thrust against Quinn, gyrating their hips together.

Quinn couldn't help a laugh, surprising himself by the way it pealed, loud and free, against the tiled walls of the shower. "I hope you'll like this. It's been years, though. Don't expect me to be an expert."

"I think I'm starting to get an idea of what you have in mind. Baby, there's no way to do this wrong."

"We'll see." Careful not to slip, Quinn began lowering himself onto his knees. The shower floor was cold and the tiles were hard, but he considered those to be only minor inconveniences. In his new position, Quinn was at mouth level with Billy's cock, which was growing stiffer by the second. Slowly, he reached out and took one of Billy's hips in a hand, and used the other to direct that prick to his mouth. He blew across the tip, flickering his tongue out to taste.

"Oh, God, Quinn," Billy groaned. "Please."

The thought of reducing Billy to incoherence excited Quinn. He took another deep breath, then slid his lips over the crown of Billy's cock and tried a suck. Billy groaned as Quinn applied suction, tasting the bitter saltiness of cock for what felt like the first time. Billy had his own unique flavor. Not sweet like some men Quinn had tasted once upon a time, but ashy, as if the cigarettes he constantly smoked affected every bit of his system. He found that he didn't mind the flavor. In fact, he liked it.

"Come on, come on," Billy urged, tangling his hands into Quinn's hair, growing wet with spray from the hot shower. "Fuck, Quinn. Oh, yeah."

Encouraged, Quinn slid his mouth a little further down. He was careful to keep his lips wrapped over his teeth—he remembered that much—but went slowly, not knowing how much he could take in. Billy's cock was just as large as he remembered, almost wider than his mouth could handle, but doable with a stretch.

Billy moaned, stumbling a little. Quinn registered the man pressing a hand against the wall to steady himself. He decided to help out by gripping both of Billy's hips, holding the man upright as he worked at pleasing Billy's cock. Careful not to startle Billy, he began, hesitantly, to use his tongue. Tentative laps at first, then, as he grew used to the texture, bolder strokes along the thrumming veins.

The hot water soaked Quinn as he sucked Billy's cock. Warm sheets of water coated him from hair to back, trickling around his knees. He closed his eyes and nursed at Billy's dick as if it held the milk of life. He wasn't thinking, deliberately not thinking, about anything beyond bringing Billy off. He'd stop and consider everything later, in due time.

Now was the time to use his mouth for something besides speech. Although clumsy, he lashed Billy's cock with his tongue, drawing off to probe at the slit, then sliding back down as far as he could. Suction while going down and coming up, faster and faster, until his head was bobbing and Billy was cursing a blue streak.

Billy's hands tightened in his hair. "Quinn," he choked. "Gonna—gonna—"

Quinn kneaded his hips, encouraging him without words. He wanted to taste Billy's come pouring over his tongue, to savor the flavor of the man's most intimate place. Humming under his breath, he sucked as hard as he could, and pressed hard with his tongue.

Oh! He'd forgotten. Removing one hand, Quinn brought it around to cup Billy's balls. In his eagerness, he squeezed a little too hard, rougher than most men would like.

Apparently, though, it was exactly what Billy needed. Throwing his head back and letting out a strangled roar, he came in a rush, flooding Quinn's mouth with bitter-salty come. No matter how long it had been, there were some things a man didn't forget, and Quinn swallowed the thick stuff automatically, savoring the taste as the come poured into his mouth in spurts.

He didn't stop working his tongue until Billy's orgasm had wrung itself dry, and then cleaned the man's cock off until there was no trace of semen left. Finished, he drew off and looked up, hoping for some kind of approval.

Billy was staring down at him with an unreadable look. Not even his eyes gave away what he was thinking. Quinn began to grow nervous and knew his own expression was faltering. "Didn't—didn't you enjoy...?"

"Come here," Billy growled. Grabbing Quinn by one arm, Billy hauled him back up to his feet. "You idiot," he mock-griped before kissing Quinn hard, a clash of mouth against his mouth. "The coming like a geyser wasn't a clue? Hell, yeah, I liked it. I'm just surprised you had it in you."

"I do now," Quinn replied seriously, then broke into a smile when Billy guffawed. Tentatively, he assayed, "And I like it, too."

"I bet you do." Billy reached up to cup Quinn's cheek. "So you want to tell me what that was all about? And don't tell me it was just returning the favor, because I know you. You wouldn't go down on someone unless you had a damn good reason. I want to hear. Spill."

Quinn searched his mind and could find no good excuse or speech, so he settled on dissuasion. "I don't know."

Billy regarded him through narrowed eyes, then nodded. "Fair enough. But never let it be said that I'm a selfish lover. You showed me a good time. My turn." His hand was suddenly grasping Quinn's cock, reminding him of how hard it was, pounding with need. Quinn gasped at the contact, a shock wave rolling through his body. "You want this," Billy said with confidence. "Let go, baby. Just feel."

His hand stroked up and down Quinn's cock, an expert touch, clever at knowing exactly what Quinn liked. Not too hard, not too easy. He touched Quinn as if cherishing him, loving the feel of his prick, fingers squeezing and dancing.

Quinn ducked his head under the spray and pressed it into Billy's shoulder. Billy made low, approving noises and quickened his tempo, jacking Quinn harder. He paused only long enough to reach down and roll Quinn's balls in his palm, teasing him with blasts of sensation, before coming back to cup Quinn's cock in his hand and working it as if it were his own.

It was hard to breathe, to think, and saying anything was completely out of the question. All Quinn could do was make low, needy noises as Billy manipulated his prick, the touch stripping him bare of anything but pure desire. His cock grew even stiffer, if that was possible, and he felt the inevitable begin to flood in.

"Billy," he managed to warn. Billy laughed, short in breath, as he squeezed hard, then flicked a thumbnail against the head of Quinn's cock.

"Come for me, baby," he ordered. The sound of his voice and the unbearably good feeling pushed Quinn over the edge. He let out a long, wordless cry as the orgasm burst through him, pushing out through his cock in long, ropy streams of come. The heavy whitish fluid splattered against Billy's legs, washed away by the water, disappearing down the drain.

Utterly without strength, Quinn collapsed against Billy. The man's strong arms surrounded him, holding him up as he himself had done earlier. Underneath the spattering of the shower water, Quinn heard Billy hushing and soothing him as his shoulders hitched. He wasn't crying, not exactly, but he felt so close to giving into tears that he might as well have been shedding them.

After a long pause, Billy helped Quinn straighten. Putting two fingers under Quinn's chin, Billy tilted his head at the right angle for a long, sweet kiss. "Good," Billy whispered into the touch of mouth against mouth. "You did so good."

Quinn basked in the praise. "Thank you," he breathed, feeling Billy's lips tickle against his own. "For...for..."

"Hush. It's okay." Billy held him close. "I know you, right? I can almost read your mind. I know what's going on in there. Don't think too hard, not right now. Just feel. Ride this roller coaster. Up or down, doesn't matter. You've got me, and I'm not letting go of you. Forget everything else. Hear me?"

Quinn had begun to shiver, but he nodded. He obeyed, just as he was accustomed to. "Billy," he breathed. "This is so much..."

"It's not *too* much. You love what I'm doing to you. Get used to it. I told you, I'm not letting you go. You're mine now." He said it with such cocky confidence that it shored up some of Quinn's doubts, all poised and ready to flood back in. "You're going to stay mine, too."

Letting go just a little, he picked up the washcloth, still soapy, from its place on the spigot and began to wash Quinn's chest. He hummed a little as he worked, making broad circles of foam between Quinn's nipples. "Good?"

"Oh, yes. Very good." Quinn stifled the voices that wanted to rush back in, shutting them up with all the sheer force of will he possessed. He'd think about things later. Right now, he was with Billy, and that was what mattered, wasn't it? "More?"

"You got it. Going to get you clean from head to toe, and then you're going to wash me." Billy moved on to Quinn's arms. His grin grew wicked. "So...what do you plan on doing today, besides classes? This week? This month? Because I gotta tell you, unless you're taken, I'm claiming you right now. You are mine. Get used to it."

Quinn closed his eyes. The warm feeling of belonging suffused his body just as the heat from the shower water eased his tense muscles, everything soothed under Billy's firm strokes with the cloth.

"I'm not doing anything else that matters," he heard himself say. "I'm yours."

For now. Yes. As long as you'll have me...I'm yours.

Chapter Ten

Quinn coughed. "Yes...I'm so very sorry. This seems to have come upon me overnight." He sneezed. "I don't want to infect any of the students." He deepened his voice into a hoarse croak. "I'll be sure to"—*cough*—"make up the material. Yes? Thank you." *Sneeze.* "Goodbye."

Billy entered the bedroom, entirely naked and wholly unconcerned. He carried a cup of Quinn's natural yogurt and a spoon shaped like a rabbit. "What the hell?" he asked as he sat down.

Quinn clicked the "off" button on his cell phone and collapsed back into bed. The sheets made a *puff* sound as he landed on them. Then, as if to apologize, they crinkled up around him like a cat rubbing against someone's legs to curry favor. He let out a breath he hadn't realized he'd been holding. Then, tentatively, he reached across to lay his hand on the top of Billy's thigh.

Billy, sitting higher in the bed with his back braced against the headboard, waved a spoon in one hand and laughed at Quinn. "You, my friend, are a shitty liar."

"I wasn't that bad."

"Yes, you were." Billy picked up his container of yogurt, beaded with condensation, and stuck the spoon in. He lifted the dripping mound to his mouth, plunged it in and immediately made a terrible grimace. "Yuck," he said around a mouthful of Light and Fit. "Now I remember why I hate this nasty-ass crap."

Quinn managed, awkwardly, to wiggle up so he sat next to Billy, shoulder to shoulder. "Give it over, then, if you don't like strawberries and cream. I'll eat the rest."

"No way." Billy pulled the container out of reach and plunked it haphazardly on his cluttered bedside table. It teetered precariously on a loose stack of magazines before gaining some measure of balance. "I don't want to kiss you and taste that shit. Speaking of which..." He reached across, angling his head, and pressed his lips to Quinn's.

Quinn surrendered to the touch of Billy's mouth with something like eagerness. He tasted of yogurt and cigarettes. Quinn's hand wanted to come up and cup the back of Billy's head, but he couldn't imagine how to do that with any degree of finesse. He contented himself instead with a brush of his far hand on Billy's stomach.

"Mmm. You're getting better at this. Now you have to work on your lying." Billy relaxed against the headboard. He reached for his cigarettes, almost upsetting the open yogurt, and fumbled for a lighter. "You don't mind, do you? Hey, maybe you'll get a real cough." He winked. "Something that stands a chance in hell at fooling someone."

Quinn kept a straight face. He'd have called himself an expert at lying, but that would bring up things he thought best kept private for the time being. Those parts of his past which Billy hadn't guessed, at least, were still his to guard. "I think the secretary believed me," he said instead. "Hopefully Ten Hawks will, too."

Billy snorted. "Bullshit. Ben's way too sharp for a fake cough, even secondhand."

"Are you complaining about my playing hooky to spend a day with you alone?" Quinn began to scratch Billy's stomach lightly, daring to be a bit playful. This felt so wicked, but incredibly liberating, albeit not a little frightening. "Perhaps I should go to my Saturday class after all."

"You better not." Billy lit up and sucked in, then expelled a thick puff of smoke. "I've got you to myself now, and we're not getting out of this bed all day long."

"Not even to dry off properly?" Quinn's hair was still dripping small droplets that ran down his arms to the pillow. Billy's own wild locks, the red still a dark magenta from the water in their shower, trailed down on his shoulders. Rivulets ran down his chest, wetting Quinn's hand.

"There ought to be a towel draped over my desk chair." Billy leaned across to hunt. "Ha!" He came up with a worn green towel with frayed edges that had almost certainly once been emerald. He laid his smoldering cigarette on the ashtray, where it sent up a thin plume of smoke. "I'll get your hair."

A part of Quinn quailed at the thought of employing a used towel, but he deliberately thrust the finicky disdain out of his head. "Thank you," he accepted instead, leaning over so that Billy could do his work. He closed his eyes in pleasure as the towel, still soft, rubbed roughly across his scalp. Billy used his fingers, scratching Quinn's roots in a way that made Quinn want to purr and curl up in his lap.

All too soon, Billy was finished. He whipped the towel away and gave Quinn a rasping knuckle to the scalp—not hard enough to hurt. Just being playful. "Now you." He dipped his head down. "I have more hair than you, so do a good job."

"Me?" Quinn held back, uncertain. He hadn't dried anyone else's hair in—well—ever. Melissa had always sequestered herself with blow dryer and curling iron until she was "presentable". In the older days, when he'd...spent time with boys his own age...they didn't bother with any such niceties, even if there was a chance to shower the morning after.

"Yeah, you." Billy butted his head against Quinn's shoulders. "C'mon, I'm still dripping and it's starting to get cold."

"Oh, now you complain." Quinn hesitantly lifted the towel. It was damp from Billy's own efforts, but it should still do. He had no idea where to start, but carefully draped the thin green terry over Billy's head. Placing his fingers just so, he began to rub at the wet hair beneath.

"Mmm, yeah." Billy undulated with satisfaction. "Harder. I can take it if you want to get rough."

"I'm sure you can," Quinn murmured. He rubbed harder, gathering the long strands up in his appropriated towel and stroking them firmly. The thin towel was soon too wet to be of use, though, and he took it away. He was startled to find himself regretful, realizing how much he'd been enjoying that. "I'm sorry. There's no more that can be done."

Billy surfaced, blinking. Quinn felt a grin tugging at his mouth, hiding a burst of laughter. Magenta streaks stuck up in every direction, leaving him with the look of a wild dog that'd just been bathed against his will. "What?" Billy asked with a frown.

Quinn felt a surge of tenderness. "Nothing," he replied, trying to keep the amusement out of his voice. He reached across and smoothed down some of the crazy cowlicks. Billy realized what he was doing and cracked up. "Sit still," Quinn scolded in amusement. "You look..."

"Yeah, I know how I must look." Billy gave his head a shake. Most of the wild locks fell back into place. "I've dried my own hair for almost thirty years now. Smart-ass. See? You're learning." He rescued his cigarette and took a puff. "Just toss the towel on the floor."

Quinn felt another flicker of dismay, but did as he'd been told. The towel landed amidst a welter of other discarded fellows, each one thin and unraveling around the edges. He liked to think they were well-loved in addition to being hard-used, and could not help but compare them to the fluffy lengths Melissa had bought him. They were still stiff after a couple months' worth of showers.

Stiff as the woman herself.

Given the choice, Quinn would opt for something worn threadbare out of affection instead of pristine perfection. Wasn't that a bit like Billy? Ragged around the edges, but comforting as a favorite blanket. Comfortable as the thin-washed sheets they lay on.

"Getting cozy?" Billy asked, nudging Quinn.

Quinn came out of his reverie with a start, realizing he'd let his head droop on Billy's shoulder. The automatic reaction was to jerk away, but he held his position for the few moments of internal struggle until they passed, and then nuzzled deeper. "Yes," he said with an almost-honest conviction. "I am."

Billy chuckled. "You feel up to another round?" He put his hand on Quinn's leg, kneading gently. "Since you canceled your class, we don't have anything better to do."

"And that's your solution to the question of an empty day, in which we could otherwise spend bettering ourselves with study?" Quinn teased, surprised at himself. "To fill the hours with sex?"

"No better way to spend a lazy Saturday. I liked your mouth on me earlier. Wouldn't complain if you went back for a second taste..." Billy pushed at Quinn's leg, his strong fingers working hard. Quinn groaned at the pleasure from the rough-and-ready massage, feeling a knot of tension dissipate under Billy's touch.

Well. It would only be fair, wouldn't it? Quinn pushed aside the momentary feeling of panic and nodded. Truth be told, he felt a hunger for the taste of that cock in his mouth again. Yogurt be damned. He'd prefer a more high-protein breakfast.

A little awkwardly, Quinn scooted down on the bed and over to one side, positioning himself at the right angle to reach with his mouth. He felt Billy's fingers slide through his hair, encouraging him. Another puff of cigarette smoke rolled over them. Quinn realized that Billy planned to smoke through this whole thing.

"Bet you can't bring me off before I finish this smoke," Billy teased. "Even if I go slow to give you the advantage."

"I don't want you to finish before the cigarette," Quinn replied. "I want this to last through a whole pack's worth."

"Now you're getting the spirit." Billy began rubbing Quinn's scalp. "Come on. Want to feel that mouth on me again."

Quinn took a deep breath. Facing Billy's cock was still new to him, but it brought back memories that suddenly seemed yesterday-clear, and an eagerness that was entirely new. He licked his lips as he gazed at the prick presented for his attention. Long and thick even when lying soft against Billy's thigh, it appealed to him far more than anything he could think of. Lying between Melissa's chilly legs had never held such appeal. He'd had to learn to like her salty taste and memorize all sorts of tricks to draw her moisture.

With Billy, it seemed all he had to do was pay attention, and his cock started to perk up. Laughing silently, Quinn positioned himself as draped over one leg, his elbow in the space between, and took a careful hold of Billy's prick. Grasping the base with his hand, he leaned in and pressed a reverent kiss to the tip of the cock he planned on fellating—no, *worshiping.*

"Yeah," Billy groaned, pushing with his hand. "Need you."

Quinn swallowed, then slid his lips over the bulbous head. Billy tasted of soap as well as musk, the slight tang of salt underlying both flavors. He sucked tentatively and was rewarded by the feel of Billy's cock swelling in his mouth. His hand tightened around the base and began slowly moving up and down, pumping Billy toward greater lengths. He sucked without finesse, but with eagerness for the feel and flavor.

There was no way to do this wrong, was there? Billy had said so. Quinn adjusted himself so that he was draped more comfortably over Billy's hard thigh, took a better grasp of Billy's cock and sucked on. He brought his tongue into play, sweeping broad, flat strokes down the length. On an impulse, he lightly scraped the silky skin with his teeth.

Billy bucked and swore.

Oh, so he liked a little pain with his pleasure, did he? Quinn tried using his teeth again, still careful to be gentle, and was rewarded with a hearty groan and a tighter grasp on his hair.

Still, it wouldn't do to overuse one trick. Quinn returned to using his tongue, learning the surface of Billy's cock as he went. He traced long veins and flicked across the head. Curious, he dipped beneath Billy's foreskin, wondering what the skin would feel like. He, himself, was cut. Melissa had approved, but now, he wondered—with a twinge of regret—what it would be like to have this much greater sensitivity.

He probed his tongue into the slit, pushing hard. Billy gasped and began shoving at Quinn's head. "Off. Come on, get off."

Quinn withdrew in confusion. He turned his head to one side and blinked up at Billy. "Did I do something you didn't like? I'm sorry."

"What are you, nuts?" Billy swore and crushed the stub of his cigarette into the bedside ashtray. "You did everything I liked, and then some. I was about to come, that's all. Decided I didn't want to pour down your throat." He spread his legs, showing off his bobbing erection. "I've got other plans for this."

Quinn's pulse quickened. He thought he had an idea of how Billy planned to use his cock. "Do you?" he asked shyly.

"Uh-huh." Billy let out a long sigh of contentment. "God, I love it when someone's as eager to please as you are. But you know, you can say no any time. Don't let me push you."

I want to be pushed. I need your direction. Quinn shook his head, knowing that the tips of his hair must have tickled deliciously. "Tell me what to do. Anything you want."

"Mmm. Come up here and kiss me, first." Billy released Quinn's hair and held his arm out. Quinn awkwardly but eagerly swarmed up into Billy's grasp, sighing in pleasure as he was caught and held tightly, hot lips on his own, a tongue demanding entrance. He surrendered gladly, letting Billy in, letting him do exactly as he pleased.

He could make Billy happy. Quinn was sure of it. Happy for...no. He wouldn't let himself think about "how long".

When Billy let go, his gaze was hot again. He slipped a hand down between them. "You hard, Quinn?" His hand closed around Quinn's cock and he grunted in satisfaction. "I thought you would be. You get off on getting other people off, don't you?"

Quinn's head bobbed on his neck and his eyes dropped to half-mast. He licked his lips and tried a smile. "Whatever you want, Billy."

"Nuh-uh." Billy frowned. "This is about what you want. So tell me. What do you want? No guessing what I have in mind. Play fair."

The command puzzled Quinn. What did he want? To please Billy. Or...did he? Completely and wholly? A desire tugged at him, an emptiness inside he longed to have filled. Did he dare?

He swallowed, steeling his nerve. "Move over," he said, giving Billy a light push. "All the way to the edge. I need the middle of the bed."

Billy laughed. "All right. Now we're getting somewhere." He moved as directed, shifting his weight until he had to stretch one leg down and brace himself against the floor. Quinn took a moment to appreciate the sight of that monster cock bobbing, then began to move. He squirmed into the center of the bed, deliberately ignoring the spatters of water from their hair and bodies, and tried to remember how this was done.

Ah. Yes.

Bracing his hands against the squeaky mattress, Quinn brought his knees up underneath himself, then raised his ass into the air and presented. As an afterthought, he parted his legs a little to further open himself. In position, he waited breathlessly to see if Billy approved.

Billy's breath grew heavy. "Oh, man, yes. This is what you want? You so got it, babe." Quinn felt a hand stroking down his leg to the knee. "Let me get the stuff."

"Hurry," Quinn dared to urge, feeling both acutely embarrassed to be so exposed, yet at the same time thrilled by the sensation. He forced his next words through shy lips. "I want to feel you inside me."

"You will." Billy pressed a kiss to Quinn's hip, darting his tongue out to trace a pattern, quick figure-eights on his skin. "I'm dying to get back in there. Just gotta get ready first. I'll make damn sure you remember me all day long whenever you park your ass."

Thrills coursed through Quinn. He wiggled, hoping Billy would hurry.

Thankfully, Billy seemed as eager as Quinn. He heard the sound of the bedside table drawer opening, and then some hasty fumbling. Billy gave a muttered exclamation of triumph as he found what he was looking for, then slapped Quinn's leg encouragingly. "You stay right where you are. My turn to get into place."

Quinn held still as he'd been directed, no matter how tempted he was to crane his head around and watch Billy. He contented himself with listening, instead, recognizing certain unmistakable sounds. The crinkling of a condom wrapper being opened, Billy's moan as he slid the latex over his cock, and then the click of a KY tube's lid.

Quinn jumped a little when he felt the first cold touch of the lubricant poured directly on the heated flesh of his ass. Billy rumbled a low laugh. "Easy, easy," he soothed. "It'll warm up." He began to use his fingers to work the slippery stuff between Quinn's ass cheeks, dipping in to tease the tightness of Quinn's hole. "God, you snap back like a rubber band. Just about choked the life out of me last time." He rubbed his thumb hard, as if leaving a stamp of approval.

When the slick fingers began to stretch him open, Quinn let out a moan and buried his face in his folded arms. His cheek pillowed against unyielding muscle, his teeth ground into his cheek and his ass burned where Billy was working away.

He couldn't have felt better.

It seemed to take an eternity before Billy was satisfied. Quinn heard the tube of lubricant clicking again, and then slithery sounds—probably Billy slicking down his own cock. "You don't need to be wet as water," he dared to tease.

"Smart-ass." Billy swatted the posterior in question. "Lube is like nail polish. More than one coat recommended." Quinn felt both hands seize his hips. "You ready for me?"

"God, yes." Quinn raised a little higher, eager for the feeling of Billy's cock splitting him open. "Hurry."

"Pushy bottom." Billy sounded breathless. "Fuck, you're gorgeous. Wish you could see yourself. Hey, wait. Wait, wait, wait."

Quinn bit back a groan of dismay as Billy scrambled off the bed. He had no idea what the man was up to, but it was delaying the coring that he wanted so badly. Gritting his teeth, he waited for Billy to find whatever he was looking for.

When he heard the *click-whirr* of an instant camera, though, Quinn jumped violently and turned around. "Billy!"

Standing naked behind the lens, Billy laughed. He took another picture. "Take it easy, babe. Just wanted one for the memories. This is prime jerk-off material."

Quinn's cheeks burned. "Billy...please. Don't." His heart pounded in his throat. "Put the camera down."

"Aw, come on. Turn that ass this way." Billy mugged for Quinn, angling back and forth. He turned the camera down to his own groin and shot a picture. He tossed it aside into a growing pile of snapshots. "I want to remember you like this."

"You won't need pictures." Quinn licked dry lips. "You'll have me around to fuck as much as you want." *For as long as this lasts... No. No. Think about that later.* "Come back to bed. Please."

Billy shot one more picture, probably out of pure cussedness, then set the camera down.

151

"Billy—don't." Quinn wanted to curl up and die from embarrassment. And pictorial proof...if he ever...one day...if Billy...

He wouldn't let himself think about it.

"Hey, easy, it's not a big deal. I'll burn them after we're done here. I was just playing around."

"You'll give me your word on that?" Quinn dared to ask.

"My hand to God. Okay, you. Assume the position." He clapped his hands and rubbed them together. "I'm coming in for a landing."

"Hurry," Quinn breathed. He relaxed a little in relief as he felt Billy climbing back on the bed, then tensed again as he felt those slippery fingers playing at his hole. Billy pushed Quinn's hips down a little, adjusting him just so, and then Quinn felt the blunt pressure of Billy's cock against his entrance.

"Yes," Quinn whispered as Billy echoed, "Yes."

His first stroke was bold, no playing around. Quinn cried out at the suddenness of the invasion, tensed up until it truly hurt, then forced himself to relax. Billy was rubbing at his back, making soothing noises. "It's okay, Quinn. Ease up."

Quinn let himself breathe for a moment, then nodded. "Go on."

"Slower this time." Billy drew back, the drag of his cock exiting exciting Quinn more than he might have thought possible. "Maybe a different angle..." Billy shifted, and thrust slowly back in.

This time, when Quinn let loose with a yelp, it was one of pure pleasure. Billy had homed in on his sweet spot again, and once it had been found, Billy wouldn't miss again. Billy grunted in satisfaction, and pushed carefully back inside.

I can do this. I want this. God, how I want this. Quinn deliberately relaxed all his muscles, opening the path for Billy's cock. Billy made another noise, one Quinn hoped was gratified surprise, and drew back, rubbing over that delicious point inside Quinn's ass. His next thrust was quicker, and his withdrawal speedy. Quinn closed his eyes, giving himself over to the ecstasy.

His lids flew back open when he felt a still-slippery hand reach underneath to grasp his cock. "Billy?"

"Shh. Gonna make you feel good."

And Billy did. Thrusting in time with his pulls on Quinn's cock, he set up a rhythm that soon had Quinn melting into a mess that tensed and loosed in turn, squeezing his body in a vise of pleasure. The feel of Billy's hand...he couldn't hold out for long. Especially when Billy paused at the end of each pump to play with the head of his cock, flicking a thumbnail across the slit.

When he came, it was with a gasp of surprise and bliss. Come spattered down in heavy drops, covering Billy's hand and creating a vast wet spot on the sheets. "Oh, yeah," Billy panted. "God, so hot. So fucking hot. Quinn, God, you move like that and I'll—I'll—"

Quinn bore down, pressing hard with his muscles. It was involuntary, but felt so very good. The iron rod in his ass jerked hard, and Billy burst out with a string of curses that should have turned the air blue. Even though there was a condom in the way, Quinn felt the blasts of semen, their heat and weight both filling the latex.

Billy slumped briefly over Quinn's back. "Damn. What do you do for an encore?"

Quinn laughed raggedly, unable to form any other words. He would have collapsed, but he didn't want to cause Billy any pain or lie in his own wet spot. "Don't need an encore," he answered honestly. "Just you..."

Billy was quiet for a moment. "Yeah," he replied gruffly. "Just you." He withdrew, then, with his usual speed of motion, jerked Quinn down to lie in his arms, spooned up against his stomach.

They'd have to get rid of the condom in a minute, but for the time being, Quinn savored the feeling of being held tightly. As if he mattered. As if he was cherished. It couldn't go on forever—*no, no, think about that later*—but he loved this. Every bit of it, from Billy's breath tickling the back of his neck, to the sweaty chest pressed against his back, to the long leg wrapping over his own.

"This feels right," he surprised himself by whispering. "You and I."

"Mmm." Billy held Quinn tighter. "That's because it is. Now shut up and enjoy the afterglow."

Quinn obeyed, pushing away every doubt and fear, letting himself surrender to the glow of orgasm. He felt lighter than air, as if he were flying—and he never wanted to come back down to earth. Billy was his only anchor, but he could soar while in the man's arms.

He felt...free.

"So," he murmured, feeling playful, "what do we do next? We have all Saturday, after all."

Billy groaned and slapped his hip. "Right now, this is fine. God, Quinn. I never thought I'd say this, but I'm glad Bitchlissa came into town. Otherwise, you might still be in that other room and I'd still be dreaming." His arms tightened. "Reality's better."

Quinn sighed in agreement. This small pocket of reality was better than anything he'd known in years.

He'd cherish it for as long as he possibly could. And then...well, he'd cope with what life threw at him next. In the meantime, he'd work on pleasing Billy as best as possible.

He could do that. He was sure of it. And he would.

Chapter Eleven

"...the question of homosexuality?"

Quinn flinched. He adjusted his position on the high stool behind his teaching lectern and wished he had a pair of glasses to take off and polish. Something—anything—to do with his hands besides lace them loosely together like a fool as the young student standing before him waited. He didn't quite dare look back at the boy's face. He was far too eager and impressionable. One wrong word could send him spiraling down the wrong path.

Quinn knew this to be true. Hadn't his own life been altered by the smallest of things?

And the largest, his inner Billy boasted. Quinn smiled despite himself.

"Dr. Whiteside?" the student asked tentatively. "Is something funny?" He fidgeted. "I mean, I know this is a lot to ask, but I figured you would be the best person to come to."

Quinn coughed. "Yes, well...I'm not sure that asking me is the wisest thing to do. You might be better off researching this on the Internet, or asking Dr. Jennings." He wiggled a little himself. "Perhaps a counselor?"

The student frowned. What was his name? "I was just asking about Oscar Wilde."

"You were? Oh." Quinn cursed himself. He'd heard the word "homosexuality" and his brain had dived down to matters at his personal hand. "Oscar Wilde...yes. A genius."

"And what society did to him was wrong," the student persisted. "He was just being himself. Right?"

Quinn glanced around and found a pencil to fiddle with. He turned it around and around in his hand as he spoke. "Society rules more of our lives than we like to acknowledge. The culture we live in influences us all in more ways than we can count. For example, it's nothing for any of us to eat a hamburger. In India..."

"What do hamburgers have to do with Oscar Wilde's sexuality?"

"Ah. Yes. We're back on that, are we?" Quinn tested the pencil's point with his thumb, not quite looking at the student. "What was your name again?"

"Josh." Josh crossed his arms. "Look, I don't mean to be rude, but are you paying attention? If you're serious about me doing some independent research, I can get behind that. Just something that'll help me add another dimension to my term paper."

"The term paper isn't due for several weeks, Josh," Quinn said kindly, although he sympathized with the young man's eagerness to do well. He'd done the same thing in more than a few classes. "We've still got a lot of ground to cover before you'd be expected to start work. And yes, we will discuss Wilde in some small part. He's not the focus, however. Austen is our primary subject of intercourse. I mean, discourse." Quinn felt himself blush at the slip. "Research on your own for a few weeks," he suggested. "I'll remind the class in plenty of time to begin their projects."

Josh looked disgusted, but otherwise kept his feelings to himself. "Okay, fine. Thanks, Dr. Whiteside."

As he turned aside, Quinn heaved a sigh of relief. It had been a week since he and Billy had begun sleeping together, and each day as he woke in Billy's arms, Quinn had promised himself that he would think about things "later". Right now he couldn't seem to bring himself to take a step back and get a logical look at the situation.

He was, simply, floating. Hovering in a bubble he didn't want to break. One wrong move and *pop*. Something would happen eventually, but until then he'd step carefully, move cautiously, and watch his words.

The one thing he knew for sure was that no one else could know. Billy hadn't pressed the issue of going public yet, although Quinn couldn't understand why. It seemed to him that Billy would be the sort who'd want to walk to the cafeteria hand in hand, or sneak into class and kiss him silly in the middle of a lecture. How would the students react to such a thing?

The pencil fell from Quinn's fingers, clattering onto his lectern, as the image filled his mind. Billy would do exactly that thing if the notion struck him. After a week of being woken by blow jobs in bed, being fucked through the mattress every night, once up against a wall, once on the floor and twice in the shower, he'd learned that when the whim struck, Billy acted.

He could see it so clearly:

The back door of the lecture hall swinging open while Quinn was using a PowerPoint presentation, pointing out key elements of *Sense and Sensibility.*

Billy walking in through the darkness, casual as if he were strolling through the gardens. Students murmuring as they recognized him.

All eyes on Billy as he ambled down to the lecture platform.

Quinn looking out into the audience and seeing him. Dropping his laser pointer from suddenly nerveless fingers.

Billy mounting the platform, grabbing Quinn by the shoulders and wheeling him around, tipping his chin up with two fingers and pressing a hard kiss to his lips.

The class would go wild. Quinn could almost hear them cheering. And as for himself? He'd stand frozen with shock for a moment, and then, unable to stop, throw his arms around Billy and kiss him back. The noise would double, some of the pupils bursting into applause...

"Professor?" a small voice broke into his fantasy. "Dr. Whiteside, do you have time to talk for a minute?"

Quinn blinked and looked down to see yet another student waiting patiently. Hasty, he swung his seating chart down to cover his lap and the erection that had half-woken. "Yes...um...Shelly?" he hazarded.

Apparently he got the name right, because she beamed. "I was just wondering if you could recommend a private tutor. I'm trying to get this stuff, really I am, but it just goes right over my head. I try to read Austen and I fall asleep."

Not the best way to endear herself to Quinn. "I'm sorry to hear that," he said a little stiffly, trying to recover some of his dignity. "I do not suggest you use the Cliff Notes, if that's what you had in mind. You'll miss out on all the subtle nuances of Austen's writing. If you're having difficulty, I suggest that you ask among your classmates for tutoring assistance."

Shelly turned slightly pink. "I was sort of hoping you could be the one to help me." She reached for a strand of honey-brown hair and began to twirl it around one finger. "I know you've got to be busy. But who gets this stuff better than you? If we spent some time together one on one...you know, just you and me...I bet I'd understand all of this in no time."

"I see." Quinn combed his memory. If he recalled correctly, Shelly had never gotten less than an A minus on any of the quizzes or tests. Her attendance had been perfect. She had an odd habit of gazing directly at Quinn during lectures... *Oh.*

"I'm sorry, Shelly, but I don't think this would be wise," he said as gently as he could. "You've been doing just fine. There's no reason to think you won't perform as well in the future."

Shelly pouted. Quinn reflected vaguely that a few weeks ago, he would have been equally as horrified at the thought of becoming involved with a student, but now he couldn't help comparing her soft, female lips to Billy's hard, manly ones.

His cock filled a bit more. Quinn squirmed. "I really am busy," he demurred, shuffling his papers out of sheer nervousness. "Here's an idea. I'll organize study groups next class. You'll be able to compare notes with others among your peers." He looked down at his lecture notes, dismissing her by refusing to meet her gaze. "I'll see you next time, Shelly."

Shelly gave a huff, but after a moment of waiting for him to look back at her—and, presumably, fall into the spell of her eyes—she turned on her heel and clattered away. Quinn *tsked* to himself and shook his head. Really, he'd developed an unhealthy dislike of heels.

He focused on his notes, ticking off everything they'd managed to cover before their allotted class period was up. They'd gotten further into the characters of *Sense and Sensibility* than he'd hoped, halfway down the cast of characters and their motivations. Quinn felt himself glowing with pleasure. The students, even if some of them were problematic, learned well for the most part. They seemed eager to learn the material. Perhaps some of them even enjoyed it, as opposed to merely wanting a passing grade.

Billy always teased him for being so intense when it came to his classes. Quinn closed his eyes, remembering Billy sprawled out on his stomach on the messy floor of his bedroom, smoking and scrawling doodles on the back of an unused quiz form. "You take this way too seriously," he'd said. "Ease up, will you? Your students are all gonna have heart attacks if you don't, first."

Then he'd grinned that irrepressible grin of his and raised up to his knees. "Hey, you on the bed. I'm talking to you, but I've got a better idea of how to use my mouth. Pants down and get on the edge."

"I've got to focus on this," Quinn had protested, but with only half his heart in the objection.

"Yeah? I want you to focus on me." Billy had grabbed his legs and pulled until Quinn was barely balanced on the bed. "Pants down, I said."

"Billy..."

"You want this. You know you do. Your mouth says no, but I see your cock jumping. Come on, baby. I'll suck you and you suck me. God, you taste good. All that health food shit must give you some kind of special flavor." He'd spread his hands wide on Quinn's thighs. "Give me what I want. You need this. Need to relax, Quinn..."

Quinn sighed. Billy had won the argument, of course. Somehow, between Billy's teasing and his own awakening libido, they'd both ended up naked and lying on the bed with a cock in reach of their lips. God, the feeling of having Billy's prick in his mouth while Billy sucked on his own dick! He'd been messy and uncoordinated, but Billy had just laughed and pushed him harder.

Every time Billy drove him into an orgasm, Quinn thought it couldn't get any better.

He was always proved wrong the next time.

Shaking his head, Quinn returned to his notes. Part of him wanted to linger on thoughts of Billy and wondering what the night at home would bring, but despite the inner devil teasing at him, he'd concentrate and get this done.

A copper-colored hand landed on Quinn's lectern. "You handled that well," a genial voice said, startling Quinn into jumping. He jerked his head up and stared into Ten Hawks' face. His heart began to pound. He hadn't talked to the Chancellor since his first week at Sweetwater, although he'd certainly heard a great deal about him from Andy during his visits.

Had he done something wrong? What warranted a personal visit from the man? Quinn felt himself grow professionally formal as he sat up straight. "Thank you," he replied, although he had no idea what Ten Hawks had approved of. "I try my best, of course."

Ten Hawks nodded. The severe lines of his face were softened by a tilted half-smile. "Shelly Roberts. She's trouble. I've had several of my male faculty complaining about her. I've put her on probation, but she just keeps trying, doesn't she?"

"Trying? Oh. Oh. I see." Quinn picked his pencil back up. "I would never dream of getting involved with a student, sir."

Ten Hawks frowned. "Don't call me that. It's Ben, or Ten Hawks if you can't stand to use my first name."

"I—I didn't mean—" Quinn stammered. "Ben. I apologize."

"Ah, well, water under the bridge now, isn't it?" Ten Hawks waved his hand. "You're probably wondering why I stopped by."

Quinn nodded, heart in his throat. *Oh, God.* What if Ten Hawks had found out about his relationship with Billy? Quinn hadn't breathed so much as a word, not even to Andy, but there were ways that things got out. If he was in for a scolding about romance on the job, it would shatter his fragile bubble. He'd have to *think* about things again.

God, but he didn't want to.

"It's no big deal," Ten Hawks said, leaning on the lectern. He patted the notes reassuringly. "You're not in trouble, Quinn. Stop looking like you've just been sentenced to the guillotine."

Quinn forced himself to breathe. "Then what warrants the occasion? Ben."

Ten Hawks shrugged. "Just checking in. I like talking with my professors from time to time to see how things are going with the semester. You'd have seen me before now, but I've been, er, busy. A little busier than I expected." He ran a finger beneath the collar of his shirt. "Things come up. You know how it is."

Blinking, Quinn took in the sight of a clearly embarrassed Ten Hawks. A late visit was no cause for—was that?—yes?—a blush. "I've heard from Andy that you've been busily occupied," he said without thinking. "Andy speaks highly of you."

Ten Hawks' color deepened. "Andy. Yes. I've spent some time with him. He's a...good man. He tells me that you and he are developing a fine friendship. That's excellent. I worried about how well you'd settle in when you were sharing lodging with someone like Dr. Jennings—Billy. But you seem to have adjusted. Andy says so, to any rate."

Quinn kept his face blank, but small exclamation points were dancing in the back of his mind. Good Lord, did Ten Hawks have a crush on Andy? Was there something in the water up here? He bit back words that wanted to come out, encouragement for Ten Hawks to go ahead and take the next step, then choked down laughter at the thought of himself, of all people, offering such advice.

He, who had yet to face... *Not yet. Not now.*

Still calm, he faced Ten Hawks. "Thank you. I have been settling in just fine. Was there anything else we needed to talk about? Ben."

"No, no, nothing else." Ten Hawks patted the lectern. "You, uh, go back to what you were doing. Talking about Andy's reminded me that I have an appointment with him in a few minutes."

"Will he come looking for you if you're late?" Quinn said, straight-faced. He kept from chuckling as Ten Hawks' eyes opened slightly wider. "He's a dedicated worker, after all."

"I'll go and find him," Ten Hawks said hastily. "Good job with the teaching. Keep on going. You'll turn out a fine batch of students. Excuse me."

Quinn watched the tall Native American hurry up the aisle of the lecture hall, neatly sidestepping the occasional piece of dropped paper or chewing gum wrapper. He managed to recover his dignity as he walked, his shoulders straightening by the time he'd reached the top of the high cement steps. Quinn watched him, amused in a vague sort of way. If Ten Hawks did have a crush on Andy, he couldn't imagine himself wishing them anything but the best.

And he certainly didn't have room to throw stones about relationships in the workplace, did he?

Quinn almost giggled, but the sound choked in his throat as the door to the lecture hall opened once more and the man of his dreams, most recently realized fantasies, stepped in easily as if he belonged there.

Billy.

Dressed casually in jeans and a sweatshirt with some faded logo plus steel-toed boots, he looked once again more like a student than a full professor. Although he was too far away for

Quinn to hear very well, he watched as Billy greeted Ten Hawks, putting a casual hand on the man's shoulder.

The pencil fell from Quinn's fingers again. He watched Billy moving casually and carelessly, his fingers kneading Ten Hawks' shoulder. He laughed about something, and managed to tease a smile onto the Chancellor's face. Instead of continuing his hurried exit, Ten Hawks lingered to laugh and chat.

Watching the two of them together, Quinn felt the first prick of the pin that would burst his bubble. *Maybe not Ten Hawks, maybe not now, but... God. I knew this couldn't last forever, yet...*

Cold, hard facts began to rush in on him. Billy wouldn't be satisfied with a shy, bumbling professor forever. Look at how he'd jumped on and off Enrique, the mover. Love them and leave them, that would be Billy's *raison d'etre*. Anyone with his lust for life would be eager to devour any morsel of pleasure that he came across. Hadn't Billy said as much once?

Ten Hawks was a lofty goal, and there was the Andy problem to consider, but Quinn could so easily see Billy charming the Chancellor into his bed. Or cozening his way into the Chancellor's bed, sucking what would no doubt be a long, thick, bronzed cock, laughing with him about things great and small, teasing him about being too serious when it came to running his university...

He'd toss Quinn aside as carelessly as a child discarded one toy in favor of the next.

And where would that leave him? Quinn's breath began to come in short, quick bursts as panic crowded in. He'd fallen off the track he'd walked so carefully for so long, all for the sake of Billy. When Billy left him, what would happen? Did he dare to try and find another man to fill his shoes, or would all the training wash over him and suck him back into a cold, sterile life filled with disdainful females? Sin and sensuality or the safe, straight path? Sex and sexuality or the straight and narrow?

His heart pounded as he watched Ten Hawks clap Billy on the shoulder, shake his head as he laughed, and head out of the lecture hall. Had they made plans to meet later? Had Billy come there to tell him it was all over?

Billy leaned against the back wall of the hall, thumbs tucked into his belt loops. His hips were thrust forward slightly, showing off his goods. Quinn couldn't stop his mouth from watering at the thought, even as he was floundering for a solid rock to cling to.

Tentatively, he raised his hand to wave. It'd be rude not to acknowledge his—former?—lover coming to visit him. He felt like a fool with his hand in the air, but kept it there until he heard the low rumble of Billy's chuckling drift down to him. Billy raised his own hand and beckoned Quinn. The message was clear—*come here.*

Without looking, Quinn shuffled his notes into a pile and stuffed them into his satchel. Slinging it over his shoulder, he began the trek up to where Billy stood waiting. Every step was accompanied by a double stab of guilt and fear. His bubble had well and truly shattered, and now he was waiting for the hammer to fall on his head.

His hands were shaking by the time he reached Billy. The expression on his face must have been one of horror, he knew, but he couldn't change it for the life of him. "Billy," he said bravely, initiating the conversation in the hopes of salvaging a little dignity. "What brings you here?"

Billy rolled his eyes good-naturedly. "You have to ask? Dumbass. C'mere." He reached for Quinn.

Quinn jumped back. "Billy, I'm not sure that's a good idea."

"Why not? No one else around. Just you and me and a great big hall. Haven't you ever dreamed about doing it in a classroom? Rolling around on the quizzes and slides?" Billy shimmied closer, winding his arms around Quinn's neck. "How about just a kiss? Got a kiss for your best guy?"

Quinn hesitated. The pause was long enough for Billy to heave a sigh and lean in to brush his mouth against Quinn's, his tongue flickering out for a brief taste. "What crawled up your butt?" he asked, still clinging to Quinn. "I know it's not me. Yet."

"I—I—" Quinn shook his head, unable to speak. He shrugged instead, knowing the gesture was inadequate.

"You, you," Billy mocked gently. "Look, you have the afternoon free, right? I've got plans for us. We can drop your stuff off at the housing and head off into the garden paths."

Quinn felt confusion beginning to cloud his mind. It dulled the fear somewhat, but raised even more questions. What was Billy's game? "What will we be doing there?" he queried suspiciously.

"You get one guess." Billy rotated his hips against Quinn's. "And maybe a couple other things."

"Billy. Outside?"

"Hell, yeah. You never did it outdoors? Damn, man, we have to remedy that. Gotta be well-rounded, right?" Billy's infectious grin lit up his face. Despite himself, Quinn began to smile. "Plus, I have food. Sex and food. Who needs more?"

"I expect you'll be taking your cigarettes along."

"See? I'm a good influence on you. You're already learning how to be a smart-ass." Billy leaned forward and kissed Quinn again, lingering this time. With his eyes closed, Quinn could almost fool himself into believing that everything was still fine, that his bubble was intact, that Billy was still wholly focused on

167

him. That he didn't have to face a future alone or with someone who didn't care...who wasn't Billy.

He kissed back as if it were the last time. Desperation lent force to his embrace, bringing his arms around Billy's back. He fisted his hands in the loose fabric of Billy's sweatshirt, grinding into the muscles beneath.

"Hey," Billy said, freeing his mouth to speak. "Something wrong, Quinn? You gotta tell me if there is, you know. I'm pretty good, but I really don't read minds."

Quinn regarded the man who'd turned his life upside down and inside out, who kept turning him on his edges, and found that he could not help but shake his head. "Nothing's wrong," he lied. "You said you had plans for us?"

"Yeah, if you dare take this outside my bedroom." Billy's eyes twinkled. "Let's live dangerously, Quinn. Never know if we'll get another chance this semester. It's warm outside and the sky is clear. We're in the middle of nowhere, with no one to see but us. Let's *live*."

The breath escaped Quinn in a long exhale. Come what might, he couldn't say no. "All right," he agreed, then dragged Billy to him for another kiss. He held on as long as he could, blocking out his own thoughts.

Perhaps he could enjoy Billy a bit longer.

If that was possible, he'd devour every morsel, just as Billy directed. He'd cherish every second before the inevitable happened.

He would, as Billy said, *live*.

Chapter Twelve

Billy, apparently, had his surprise laid out on part of one of the nature trails. Quinn couldn't have said he was startled. Billy had specified "outdoors", and where else would he go unless they headed into the actual hills? This was dangerous, as any professor or student could come along at any minute, but at least—for which Quinn was devoutly grateful—they weren't in the backyard of the faculty housing.

Quinn looked carefully around himself, taking in the details of the glorious autumn colors on the trees, gently falling leaves and beams of sunshine arrowing through gaps in the foliage. Billy seemed to shine, bathed in a perpetual glow as he moved. His skin was as beautifully bronzed as it had been when they first met, and except for a few inches in length, his magenta-tipped hair hadn't changed. The locks gleamed as if tipped by rubies. His lips were soft and full, begging to be kissed. While gazing, Quinn caught a glimpse of Billy's bright blue eyes sneaking a peek at him in return, and blushed, realizing that he'd been staring like a wide-eyed child.

Hastily, to cover his lapse in manners, Quinn asked, "Where are we going?" Billy hadn't specified much, and he carried a bulging knapsack that couldn't help but arouse curiosity.

"I told you, it's a surprise. You'll see." Billy winked at Quinn. He sparkled with mischief as he reached out and took Quinn's hand, boldly linking the two of them together.

Quinn almost managed to restrain his flinch, but couldn't stop himself from glancing around to see if anyone were watching.

Billy frowned. "Hey, what have I told you about chilling out? You're thinking again." He came to a stop as Quinn cringed, the fear of being scolded springing up like a tight fist in his chest.

But instead, turning Quinn so that they faced each other, Billy brought his hand up to lightly touch Quinn's cheek. "No one's around. It's just you and me out here. Promise. Okay?"

Quinn swallowed down his uneasiness. After a moment of careful listening, when he didn't hear anything or anyone else but a few late-season birds, he nodded. "Okay," he added, just to be sure.

Billy's broad grin was a welcome reward for compliance. He turned back around facing forward, gave their joined hands a little shake, and began to walk again. "We don't have far to go now. You're gonna love this."

Quinn wasn't at all sure that he would, but he'd been swept up in Billy's wake. He followed behind like a seashell in the tide, unable to stop the pull on his hand or his senses or his... No, he wouldn't say heart. That was too dangerous.

Especially now, when he'd come to the conclusion that Billy wouldn't be a lasting part of his life. The man might be satisfied with quiet, bumbling Quinn for a time, certainly, but Quinn knew he'd end up boring Billy stiff. He had only to look around himself to see the proof of that. For example, Billy saw a beautiful day of Indian summer and a chance to have some fun.

Quinn saw the beauty, yes, but he also saw endless possibilities for getting into trouble.

Why would Billy hang around to hold Quinn's hand forever?

Stop thinking. Do what Billy's told you time and time again. Just feel. This is a gorgeous day, one to be savored, and you should cherish the moments you have left. Billy would tell you to drain each second dry. Do that. You'll have memories to keep you warm when he's gone.

Tentatively, Quinn squeezed back, flexing his fingers in Billy's. Billy tossed him a grin and shook their hands again, swinging to and fro as if they were children on a playground. However, there the similarity stopped. Quinn knew that Billy would be bent on some very adult games once they arrived at—wherever it was.

"Okay," Billy said, coming to a stop. He extricated their hands from their grip together and pointed at what looked like a thinly worn footpath through a tangle of trees that lined the nature trail. "It's just through here. I found this place a while ago. I don't think anyone ever goes there. Pretty sure, anyway."

"Pretty sure," Quinn echoed. He licked his lips. Well, the small path would be hard to spot if one were casually ambling down the trail. You'd have to look for the thing to find it. It should be safe...should be. Folding his arms across his chest and running his hands over his biceps, he inclined his head in agreement. "All right."

Trusting Billy was so chancy. But he—he wanted to play the game out, no matter how uncomfortable it might make him on occasion.

Didn't he?

Yes, he told himself, discovering it to be the truth. *I've told Billy that I am his, and yes, I want to be. I realize that means stepping beyond the boundaries of what I'm not comfortable with, but he's such a vibrant force of personality that one cannot help being attracted to him.*

No…take that down to a personal level. I, Quinn, am attracted to Billy. Perhaps I always have been from the moment I first met him. So charismatic, so full of joie de vivre, so very much the bon vivant. He's everything I've ever wished, in my secret dreams, of being. Everything my fantasies have wanted, when I've allowed myself the luxury.

Billy can take me out of myself, if I let him. He can shape me into an entirely different person. Already I feel the changes in the air and beneath my skin.

He's teaching me how to know myself. For as long as this lesson lasts, I'll savor it.

This much I swear.

"Quinn? Hey, Quinn, you in there?" Billy was snapping his fingers in front of Quinn's face. Quinn blinked, then realized he'd gotten lost in his thoughts…while staring vacantly at Billy's impish face. "Jeez, I know I'm pretty, but you've gotta stop this moony-eyed gazing shit. It'll go to my head." He laughed. "So, you ready to brave the wilderness?"

Billy held back a branch on the side of the trail. "I'll go first. You can follow behind me. It's not far, but watch your step, okay? There are some briars and I don't want you getting hurt."

Quinn felt a small flush of pleasure. Billy cared. "I'll look where I step," he said obediently, gratified by Billy's look of approval. "This way?"

"Yep. Just step where I do, and you'll be all right." Billy took his first stride off the trail, ducking underneath the raised branch and holding it up for Quinn. Quinn swallowed and followed in Billy's footsteps, feeling as if he were doing something far more dangerous than simply diverting from a common road.

Dangerous...and exciting.

The trek through the woods was, as Billy had promised, not very long. Quinn remained watchful as to where he put his feet, and only got snagged on a string of thorns once. Billy teased Quinn as he got them untangled from Quinn's pants, finishing up with a light slap on his calf.

And when they emerged, it was in a little piece of paradise.

Billy stood at the edge of the small clearing they'd walked into and beamed. "Well? What do you think?"

Quinn shook his head. The place they stood in wasn't wide—perhaps eight feet across and equally broad—but there were no rocks, no briars and no tree stumps. The ground was covered by a mat of crackling autumn leaves in every fall color there could be, looking soft as a downy pillow. Billy took on an entirely new aspect as he stood in the middle of nature. An almost fox-like glow. He seemed one-hundred-percent at home.

Quinn felt that he himself must have stuck out like a sore thumb. Nevertheless, he appreciated the wild beauty of the place. "Where did you find this? I mean, how?"

Billy chuckled as he swung the knapsack off his shoulder and set it down next to one of his legs. "A couple months ago I was looking for a good place to bring someone. This was perfect for what I needed. Quiet, secluded, no chance of being interrupted..." He turned so that Quinn could see him waggling his eyebrows. "Perfect little seduction spot, huh?"

Quinn felt himself begin to grow warm. "Yes," he agreed. "Is that...seduction is what you plan on?" He hoped, but didn't quite dare to presume. Then again, given that this was Billy, it would be a safe wager that sex was what he had on his mind.

"If you play your cards right. Come on, sit down. If you get dirty, it'll wash." Billy folded down into a cross-legged position and patted the leaves in front of him. "Get comfortable."

Quinn hadn't sat on bare earth in more years than he could remember. All the same, it felt somehow right to be following Billy's lead. And, as he carefully lowered himself, it wasn't awkward or off-putting. The leaves crunched underneath him, welcoming as a blanket could be.

He smiled at Billy, the expression neither false nor forced. "This is nice," he said honestly, hoping that Billy would be able to read the nuances of his simple statement. "I like it here."

Billy's grin broadened. He ran a hand through his hair, tangling a bit on the magenta tips, and looked almost bashful. "You're the first guy besides me to set foot in this place. I was kinda glad when I remembered never having brought anyone else up here. Wanted this to be a special place for us."

The warm glow suffused further through Quinn. "Thank you," he said, putting some of that gentle heat into his voice— again, without deliberate effort or in an attempt to win favor. "I'm glad you thought of this, then."

"Yeah. Me too." Billy ducked his head and reached for his knapsack. Quinn watched him as he moved, imagining the play of muscles underneath Billy's sweatshirt, remembering how they felt under his own two hands. What hadn't they done together? Very little. This was new...and surprisingly exciting. He found himself eager to see what Billy had stashed in his sack.

The first thing that came out was a thin ground blanket, gaudily checkered and stiff, but new-looking, as if Billy had bought it just recently for this very purpose. Billy unfolded the thing and frowned. "Looked bigger on the label. C'mon, give me a hand."

Quinn reached out to help. Between the two of them, they got the small square of felt unfolded and spread roughly beside them. Billy nodded in approval. "Okay, next, food." He produced two apples, harvest-red and rosy ripe, plus a small knife, and laid them on the blanket. "You hungry?"

Quinn chanced honesty again. "Not really. I suspect I may be working up an appetite in a bit, though."

Billy hooted as if surprised. "Man, you really are coming along great." He reached across to pat Quinn's shoulder in approval. "Don't change too much, though, huh?" he asked, smoothing the pat into a caress. "I kinda like you the way you are."

Quinn felt himself turn pink. "I can't imagine..." he began, then stopped himself. How could Billy like him the way he was? No, it couldn't be.

"Try to," Billy said, then leaned forward for a kiss. Quinn closed his eyes as their lips met, and for a change was the first to put out his tongue for a deeper embrace. Billy made a small noise that Quinn couldn't interpret but opened up all the same. Quinn swept in, tasting the flavors of cigarettes and man, the combination unique to Billy himself, and loving them.

Billy pulled away with a grin. "Someone ate his Wheaties." He leaned back neatly, bracing himself with his arms, and sparkled across at Quinn. "What else do you have cooking in that big brain of yours? Something I'll like?"

Quinn bit his lip. He'd had a wild idea flash through his mind...something he hardly dared even think about...but why not? Billy would encourage him if he knew what was in Quinn's thoughts, Quinn was sure, and if this was truly going to be one of their last times together, then he ought to make the most of it.

"I think so," he replied, getting back up to his feet. "Billy, move over to the blanket, if you will?"

Billy chortled. "Okay. Gotta say I like this side of you." He moved as directed, settling himself on the stiff fabric with another crunch of leaves. Leaning back again, he looked up at Quinn and tilted his head in curiosity. "Now what?"

"Now," Quinn said, gathering his courage, "you start to sing. Anything you like, so long as it's slow and...sexy." He stumbled a bit over the last word, but got the syllables out. "Please."

"I have a feeling I'm really gonna like this." Billy twinkled at Quinn, then sat thinking for a moment. Finally, he began to vocalize an old jazz riff, something that made Quinn think of smoky clubs, vodka tonics and days gone by when everything illicit was a deep thrill.

Quinn took a deep breath and reminded himself that he wanted to do this. It was daring, but it felt good in his own mind to be this bold, this wild, this free. Billy's lessons were sinking home, and he felt like he glowed with the new awareness of self. He'd take small steps, but confident ones.

And he hoped that Billy would understand the meaning behind what he chose to do. That Billy would know this wasn't for just him, but for Quinn as well.

Billy continued to sing, patiently waiting for Quinn to begin. He had a broad grin on his face, as if he'd clued in to what was about to happen, but was content to let Quinn move in his own good time. Observing this, Quinn felt something inside him settle. *Yes. It's time.*

Carefully timing himself with the slow, sultry rhythm of Billy's vocalization, Quinn moved his hands up to the buttons on his shirt. One by one, he undid them, the cool air and sunlight striking his skin at the same time.

Billy changed his tempo to something with a deeper pulse and sat forward. He made a waving motion, encouraging Quinn to keep on going. Almost laughing at his own daring, Quinn did so. He untucked his open shirt and let it hang down around his legs, framing his groin. His cock, which had begun to swell, outlined in his pants.

Quinn reached down and stroked himself, rubbing through the layers of his khakis and boxer shorts. The touch felt surprisingly good—and equally freeing, as if he were shedding a layer of something heavy that had lain across his shoulders. He hadn't been this bold in ages, but it was...wonderful. He caressed his cock harder and nodded to Billy.

Billy didn't miss a beat of the song as he reached down and began to rub his own growing bulge. Quinn's mouth all but watered at the thought of what lay behind his zipper. "Let me see," he asked, amazed at his daring but delighted at the same time. "Lie back and pull it out."

"Pull what out?" Billy stopped singing long enough to ask.

Quinn chose his words like jewels in a golden case. Each one glittered. "Your cock. I want to see."

"All you had to do was ask." Gracefully as an oversized cat, Billy stretched himself out on the blanket and ran a hand down his stomach. He pushed up his sweatshirt to reveal an expanse of honey-brown skin, and reached for the zipper on his jeans. Quinn paused in his own movements to watch, fascinated. Billy opened the denim and pulled his cock out, already more than half-hard, with no underwear in the way. As he started singing again, he began to jack himself off, fingers trailing up and down his shaft.

Quinn felt almost like he wanted to laugh. Not at Billy, not in a mean spirit, but for pure glee. God, but it was wonderful to be so free of cares. How had he lived for so long without giving in to these urges? Seeing and being seen. Touching and being touched. The simple joys.

He felt as if he'd been given a drink of water after passing through the desert. And for all this, he had Billy to thank. Billy, who could be counted on to take Quinn in his arms after Quinn had finished stripping, who'd roll him over onto his back, take supplies from that knapsack, and fuck him through the forest floor. *God...Billy.*

Quinn reached for his own zipper, fingers toying with the small tab. He laughed a little as Billy sang, feeling happy as he could be. The zipper slid down smooth as quicksilver. He reached for the waistband of his pants and boxers, ready to push them down.

"Quentin, what in God's name are you doing? Stop that at once!"

Quinn's blood froze in his veins. He knew that voice. Knew it all too well. Billy stopped singing and sat upright a little. He scowled darkly at the person behind Quinn. "What the fuck are *you* doing here?"

Quinn's hands fell to his sides. "Hello, Ms. Rife," he said without turning. "What brings you out here this afternoon?"

"Quentin, really. You know my given name as well as your own. We are all but engaged, aren't we? Call me Melissa."

"Bitch-lissa," Billy scoffed.

"Billy, don't." Quinn felt curiously calm. Everything in and around him had gone still, waiting for him to make his next move. "Don't speak to her, please."

"I'll say what I want when I want when that woman's come around to try and brainwash you again." Billy's eyes pled with Quinn. "I just want to keep you safe."

"I doubt that to be your intention. And put that—that *thing* away before I report you for public indecency." Melissa's tone was full of scorn. "What kind of game are you playing with my Quentin?"

"It's not a game, Melissa," Quinn said without ire. He refrained from turning around to face her. "Please don't make a scene in front of my company."

Melissa gave a sharp *tch* of startled irritation. "I have no intention of doing any such thing. Although I do also hope you have an explanation for this."

Quinn heard a staccato thud, as if Melissa were tapping her shoe on the leaves. They went *crunch, crunch, crunch* as she increased her pace—a sure sign, he knew, of her growing impatience.

For his own part, he felt still as a waveless ocean.

"Well? Quentin?" Melissa demanded.

"Ms. Rife, I suggest that you turn around and walk out of this clearing." Quinn's hands went to his fly. He zipped his pants back up. Though it took some effort, especially as he could feel Melissa's cold gaze burning a hole through his back, he remained in place, facing Billy. "Don't listen to anything she says."

"As if I would," Billy snorted. He lay there exposed, his erection going down but his temper clearly up. "So, what? You heard a few rumors or something? Decided whoever-you-were-fucking wasn't enough? Had to come back down here and try to get your Quinny-bear?"

"I never lost Quentin," Melissa replied flatly. "We had a disagreement, yes. I never thought he'd do something quite this foolish, although I shouldn't have put it past him. Our regime was very thorough."

"Regime." Billy made a disgusted sound. "So you were the one jerking his deprogramming strings?"

"I knew he'd had deviant urges before he embarked on a successful regime of therapy," Melissa corrected. "However, he'd been *clean* for some time before we met. Quentin, turn around and look at me. Quentin, are you deaf? I told you to turn around."

Quinn's lips were going numb. "Ms. Rife, I've asked you once to leave. Please don't make me repeat myself."

"Quentin, you'll make me genuinely angry if you don't stop this nonsense at once. Turn around."

"No," Quinn heard himself say. "I'm staying right where I am, and you're going to leave."

"I most certainly am *not*. Quentin, you're coming with me. I've reserved a room in the bed-and-breakfast where we stayed the last time I was in town—"

"Where you stayed," Billy sneered. "He was home with me, getting fucked six ways to Sunday."

"And your point is? He's clearly slipped off the treads, but if you're the only negative influence in his life I can easily turn him back around."

"I do have a name, you know," Quinn said quietly.

Both Billy and Melissa ignored him. Billy sat up, stuffing his cock into his pants and zipping them shut. "So you ride back into town, all set up on your high horse, and he's supposed to wind himself back around your little finger? Nuh-uh, lady. He's mine and I'm not letting go."

"I had him first. He belongs to me."

"I'm not a possession," Quinn whispered.

"Yes, you are," Melissa snapped. "You are a commodity. A valuable asset. A potentially distinguished professor of literature will make a fine husband for the successful lawyer I plan to become. An intended life partner I don't intend to lose. I came down here to talk some sense into you. It wasn't hard to find out where you'd gone. And when I heard the singing, I knew where to look. Quentin, turn around and face me at once."

"No."

"That's right," Billy said, getting to his feet. "The man's mine, bitch. Give up. I win, you lose, and you go home now." He made a shooing motion with his hands. "Run along."

"Quentin, come with me."

Quinn felt Melissa's cold hand touch his arm. She took a firm grip and tugged. "My patience is not indefinite."

"Yeah, I'd say it had a pretty short lifespan, given that you were fucking someone else just a couple months after Quinn came down here to teach." Billy grabbed Quinn's other arm. "Get out of here, cunt."

"Quentin! Do you plan on standing there like a statue without defending my honor? Answer me at once. This person has just insulted me. What do you say to him?"

"The same thing I'll say to both of you," Quinn replied slowly before wrenching both of his arms loose. "I'm not a thing for you to own or trade. I'm a person."

Melissa made a noise of surprise. "Quentin, be reasonable."

"I am. For the first time in years." Quinn took a deep breath, deeply shocked at his own behavior but unable to stop the words tumbling from his lips. How many years had it been since he'd listened to his heart, uninfluenced by anyone or anything else? "Go home, Melissa. You too, Billy. If you both don't leave, I will."

"Quinn..."

"Quentin..."

"I warned you," Quinn said flatly. "Go to hell. I can't—I won't—"

Leaving his sentence unfinished, he turned and fled into the trees, tearing a rough path through the woods, leaving both of his anchors behind.

Flying without a safety net and terrified out of his wits.

CR03ЄO

Quinn didn't get very far before he stopped, running just as long as he continued to hear raised, angry voices behind him. When he could hear nothing but birds, crackling leaves and his own heaving breath, he came to a stop. It wasn't the exertion so much as the emotional turmoil that had him gasping for air.

Bending over a tree stump, he was noisily sick into the undergrowth.

When his stomach had stopped heaving, Quinn dragged a shaking hand across his mouth and wished for something to take away the sour taste of vomit. Mints. Did he have any mints in his pocket? A quick fumble proved that he did. Thrusting two into his mouth, he sucked hard on the pastilles until his mouth lost that metallic tang.

He needed to sit down. Stop his legs from shaking. Try to gather his wits about himself. Where, though? No place handy but the ground. Or wait...just a little further in. A fallen tree, its trunk round and rough, but a good enough place to rest. A few paces on shaky legs brought him to the spot he'd chosen. Using a branch for leverage, he sat down hard and sank his head into his hands.

Oh, God. How badly had he fouled things? But for Melissa to come back into his life...and for Billy to fight for him...why had it seemed wrong for Billy to claim him so boldly, when Quinn had been willingly giving himself to the man? Quinn didn't understand. He felt as if he should have been standing next to Billy and telling Melissa to fuck off with just as much fervor.

Melissa. God, Melissa. If there hadn't been a Billy, he would have jumped for joy to see her walking back into his life. He'd clung to her for so long, but once he'd seen her true colors—shocking, ugly colors—he found that he couldn't blind himself once more to their stain. Melissa stood out like a dark and oily patch in his recent past.

And Billy? Billy had been a patch of clear blue sky. He'd felt so free and alive when he was with his fellow professor. Billy was the one Quinn wanted to be with, the man he'd been desperate to hold onto until Billy let him go.

Yet when Billy had claimed him, Quinn had been the one to flee.

Quinn ground the palms of his hands into his eyes, groaning as his vision filled with sparkles. What was going on? Why had he reacted the way he did? He didn't understand in the slightest and doubted that he would.

But if he had a choice? If there was a way to go backwards in time, what would he do? Quinn rubbed harder, thinking. *I don't know. I couldn't bear to have them both tugging at me like a rag doll, pulling as if they would tear me in half.*

Billy is the one I want, not Melissa.

Or do I?

Quinn removed his hands and sat upright. Perhaps it wasn't so much Billy that he wanted as he did a chance to be himself again. He'd been a fool when he was young, but did it necessarily follow that he would have continued to be foolish as he grew? What would have happened if he hadn't gone into the deprogramming?

A life unlived folded out in front of Quinn's mental vision. He would have been confident, easy and free, laughing at the excesses of youth while adjusting himself to being a confident adult. He had the feeling that if he'd stood his ground back then, he would be a much happier man now.

You can't change the past. All you can do is look toward the future.

But what would the future hold if there was no Billy in it? No Melissa? No anchors, no rocks?

Quinn took a shuddery breath. He suspected he'd have no choice. He'd ruined his relationship with Billy, and the thought of going back to Melissa or any other female left him feeling cold and uneasy.

It felt frightening to think, but he had been right. He wasn't a possession. He was a man, a full professor, and he should know his own mind. Not belonging to anyone didn't mean he was all alone.

It merely meant that he had to find his own way. What that would be, he didn't know.

But he could find out. Make his own choices. He could depend on himself.

And, by God, he *would*.

Quinn tilted his head to the side and listened. Still nothing beyond birdsongs and falling leaves. Perhaps Melissa and Billy had both left. He couldn't return to the apartment, but he had enough for a night's stay at a motel down in town. Perhaps several nights' stay. He could begin looking for an apartment. Andy might not mind a roommate who'd keep quiet about certain visitors.

For the first time ever, the thought of facing life on his own terms didn't frighten Quinn. He marveled at the notion, tested it from all angles, nearly poked it with a stick, and tentatively...tentatively...accepted it.

He could be his own man. And he'd start with finding his way out of the forest, back down the nature trails and off for the town. He didn't need Melissa. He didn't need Billy.

But God help him, he still *wanted* Billy. Even if he couldn't have him anymore. Perhaps especially because of that.

Heaving a deep sigh, Quinn started to get up—then stopped. He heard the sound of crunching leaves and undergrowth being stepped on. Someone was coming his way, walking with a heavy stride. It could be Melissa in a furious temper...or it could be Billy, with red in his eye.

An hour before, Quinn would have been terrified and desperate to avoid a confrontation. Now, he simply sat on his tree bench and waited for the person to become visible through the forest. If it were Melissa, he'd tell her the truth without embellishment and send her on her way.

If it were Billy...?

He didn't know.

"Quinn?" a male voice called, rough around the edges from too much smoking. "Quinn, come on. It's going to get dark soon and it'll be freezing up here."

"I can take care of myself," Quinn said with the same inner calm he'd found during the previous argument. "I'm a grown man, Billy."

"There you are." Billy crashed through the brush, cursed when he hooked himself on some briars, untangled his jeans and stomped over to Quinn. "You just about scared the shit out of me."

Quinn looked up placidly. The bark was beginning to bite into his behind, but he sat as easily as if he had all day and nowhere else to go. "I didn't mean to," he said honestly. "I had to get away. That's all."

"Damn, Quinn." Billy thrust his hands into his pockets and looked lost. "I thought up a dozen different things that could have happened to you out here. What if I hadn't been able to track your path?"

Quinn glanced at the rack and ruin he'd made during his flight. "I suspect that finding me wasn't any too difficult."

"Yeah. Right." Billy laughed shakily and dragged a hand through his hair. "Quinn, man, please don't do that again. My heart can't take it."

"What does your heart have to do with anything?" Quinn frowned. "Surely you weren't that concerned over my well-being."

"Jesus, Quinn! If I didn't love you I'd smack you across the head. Shit, I'm half-tempted as it is." Billy paused, then stuck out his chin. "Yeah, I said it. Doesn't matter if you don't feel the same way. I love you."

Quinn felt as if he'd been struck by lightning. "But you...why...how can you?" he asked faintly, unsure of his words once again. "Why would anyone love me?"

"I really am gonna smack you now. Move over." Billy gestured with his hands. Too stunned not to obey, Quinn made room for Billy on the trunk.

Billy sat, then turned at the waist so he faced Quinn. Quinn mirrored his actions, still peaceful at the center but burning with curiosity. Billy loved him? How was that possible? Billy, the playboy? Billy, who put the one into one-night-stand?

They sat in silence for a moment. Billy appeared to be struggling for words. "Quinn...it hasn't been long, I know. At least since we've been together. I've watched you for months, though. Waiting. Wanting. And when I finally got you, when you gave yourself to me, it went to my head."

"I did what you wanted because I needed you," Quinn replied. He folded his hands in his lap. "You were there for me when I didn't think I had another friend in the world."

"That's the thing. I've just realized...Quinn, man, it doesn't matter how *I* feel. The biggie here is how *you* feel. Don't say 'yes' or 'I love you' because you think I want to hear it." Billy reached across and took Quinn's hands in one of his own. "If you want to go back to being someone else, if that'll make you happy, then do it. No more going by what other people think or say."

Quinn shook his head. "I'm not going to," he said clearly. "I'm going to live my own life. Billy, do you know that up until the moment when Melissa arrived, I had thought you would be the one to leave me? And until now, I thought I'd lost you forever? How do you think I felt?"

"Like shit. And that's my fault, mostly." Billy released Quinn's hands to reach up and run his fingers through Quinn's hair. A smile tugged at his mouth. "Bet this is the longest you've ever let it grow."

"In a few years." Quinn regarded Billy frankly. "I can't say 'I love you' yet, no matter how much I might want to. How much I might feel... Can you understand that for me?" He leaned over to kiss Billy lightly. "I do, you know. But I've always been the cautious type."

Billy laughed, then nodded. Quinn approved. Billy clearly respected Quinn enough not to press him. Quinn still felt dizzy at the thought that Billy would want to stay with him. It was too big, too much.

Yet at the same time...it wasn't a bad thing. It felt like a very good thing. One he could get used to. Couple that with his new determination to live life as he saw fit, and the pieces melded together.

Cautiously, Quinn turned so he faced Billy, mirror images of one another. A shy and clumsy neophyte across from a self-assured, well-practiced Don Juan. Both of them caught up in the same uncertainty.

The look of concern on Billy's face was more touching than a thousand words.

Quinn lifted both his hands and placed them on either side of Billy's jaw. He went slowly, so he could be stopped if Billy didn't want this, and kissed the man. Billy went rigid for a second, then melted into his embrace. Quinn took the lead for the second time that day, doing things the way he wanted them done.

When they parted, Billy had the ghost of his old cocky smile on his face. "Does that mean you'll give me a chance?"

"That depends. What did you do with Melissa?"

"I wrung her neck and stuck her in a knothole."

"Good." Quinn paused before grinning, himself. "What actually happened?"

Billy shrugged. "She went off in a huff, ranting about sin and damnation. She might be back. I don't know."

"I can handle her. She doesn't like anything that she's controlled to slip out of her grasp—which is, no doubt, why she came after me. But we never signed any papers. If she persists, she'll be thought of as an obsessive lunatic. She won't want any tarnish on her reputation. Odds are that if I go on as I've just now begun, she'll distance herself as far from me as possible." The thought was positively delightful. "I, on the other hand, can afford to be unorthodox." He chuckled at the word he'd chosen. "And I can be with you, if I want."

"Do you?" Billy's blue eyes were filled with apprehension.

"I think I do," Quinn said after a moment's pause. "I don't know how long this will last, Billy. Perhaps you *will* grow tired of me, or I of you. But we can play the game until we either run out of cards or decide to stand firm. I think I can cope with this now." He leaned in to kiss Billy again, running his tongue along the man's bottom lip. "I want to."

Billy laughed. "Okay. We face the future together. Equals." He stood and offered Quinn a hand. "But I'm still the top."

Quinn's laughter rang out into the night. Full, honest...and free.

About the Author

Willa Okati has a hundred and one different stories to tell, and she's getting there one book at a time. Permanently glued to her computer chair or parked in front of a laptop, she can be found pounding the keys from before dawn until after dusk. She's delighted to have found a home at Samhain where she can write her Appalachian-with-a-twist paranormal stories. Coffee is her best friend and her lifesaver; cats are her muses; her bookshelves are groaning under the weight of a tremendous collection.

She'd love to hear from readers, and can be contacted at willaokati@gmail.com. Drop her a line anytime or join her Yahoo! group to join in the fun with other readers as well as Willa. http://groups.yahoo.com/group/willa_okati/. You can also find Willa on MySpace at http://blog.myspace.com/willaokati.

Look for these titles

Now Available

A Year and a Day
Unspoken
The Letter
Café Noctem
Sex and Sexuality
Hearts from the Ashes

Coming Soon:

*Mountain Magic (paperback collection of A Year and a
Day, Unspoken and The Letter)*

Love is the journey of a lifetime.

Love's Evolution
© *2006 Ally Blue*

Chris Tucker is a cultured and sophisticated gentleman. Matt Gallagher is a pierced and tattooed wild child. Not exactly the pair you'd expect to become a couple. But the sparks fly between them from the moment they meet, and the fire never goes out.

Through the first rush of attraction to falling in love, through jealousy and sexual experimentation and a life-threatening injury, the bond they share grows and deepens. Come along with Matt and Chris on their journey, and share their joys and heartaches, from their first hello to happily ever after and everything in between.

Available now in ebook and print from Samhain Publishing.

Enjoy the following excerpt from Love's Evolution...

It was after midnight by the time the last of the guests left. Laurie raised an eyebrow and grinned as she hugged Chris goodbye. Chris watched her retreating back nervously. The woman was far more perceptive than he liked sometimes.

Rick offered to stay and help clean up, making sure he said it loud enough for the exiting partygoers to hear.

"Dude, don't worry," Matt said. "Nobody's gonna think anything of it if you stay." He gave Rick a sharp pop on the butt and grinned up at him.

"Yeah, well. Okay, yeah, so I'm a little nervous." Rick laughed. "Stupid, huh?"

"Naw. I bet Chris is more nervous that you. Aren't you, babe?"

Chris nodded as he doused the final torch and headed back up the steps to the deck, where Matt and Rick were picking up trash. "I must admit, I am a little nervous."

"See, I told you." Matt shook his head. "Sad. You guys are so hot for each other, but I bet I'm gonna have to work you both like a porn fluffer before you get going."

"Matt, really..."

Matt laughed. "Hey, I was just kidding, Chris." He wrapped both arms around Chris's waist and kissed the end of his nose. "C'mon, relax, will you? It's nothing to worry about." He flicked his tongue over Chris's lips. "Just sex, baby, that's all. Just a little bit of sin. It's good for you."

Chris smiled. "That's not what I learned in Sunday school."

"There are degrees of sin, Chris." Matt sucked Chris's bottom lip into his mouth for a second. "This is just a little one. If you believe in that sort of thing, that is."

"Matt, my darling, I know you don't believe in sin, raging atheist that you are."

"Look who's talking."

"You're a raging hedonist too."

"It's still not wrong, Chris."

"I agree with you, it's just...I don't know. I'm just nervous. So's Rick."

Rick kept his gaze fixed on his feet and didn't say anything. Matt frowned.

"Look, nobody has to do anything they don't want to here, right? If you guys have changed your minds, that's fine. It's no big deal."

Chris stared hard at Rick. His hair hung thick and shining over one eye and caught on his full lower lip. The lean muscles in his arms made Chris's skin ache.

"No. I haven't changed my mind." Chris reached out and brushed his fingers across Rick's wrist. "Rick?"

Rick moved closer and wound an arm around each of them. "I still want to." His long fingers slid into Chris's hair, and Chris leaned into the caress.

Matt smiled. "Let's go inside now." Taking their hands, he led them into the house.

They followed in silence. Matt snagged an almost full bottle of Shiraz off the kitchen counter and brought it along to the bedroom. Upstairs, Chris sat on the padded window seat and gazed out at the moonlit yard.

"It's a lovely night," he said.

"Sure is." Rick walked over and sat beside Chris.

"Matt, do we have any condoms?" Chris asked. "Not to kill the mood, but frankly, I can't remember the last time we used any."

"I got some last week." Matt shuffled through a pile of CDs on the built-in shelves. "Just in case, you know. But we don't have to use 'em if you don't want. Rick's clean. We shared test results yesterday."

Chris gaped at Matt, then Rick. Rick had the good grace to blush. Matt gave Chris a sweet smile that he knew from long experience to be pure deception.

"Okay," Chris said. "I suppose it's a good thing that you two have already discussed this."

"Hey, we're pretty responsible guys when we feel like it." Matt popped a CD into the portable player and jungle drums sounded through the room.

"What the hell's that?" Rick asked.

Matt shrugged. "Some sort of Polynesian music I downloaded the other day. I kinda like it, it's sexy." Digging some matches out of a drawer, Matt started lighting the candles Chris kept scattered around the room. He took a long swallow of Shiraz, then held the bottle out. "Want some?"

"Yeah, give it here." Rick took the bottle Matt offered, drank, and passed it to Chris.

The urge to tease was strong, and Chris saw no reason to question it. Holding Rick's gaze, he ran his tongue along the rim of the bottle and dipped it briefly inside before drinking. Rick's cheeks flushed pink.

Matt nodded. "Yeah, that's it. Damn, I'm getting hot just watching you guys flirt."

Rick laughed. "If you're so hot, why don't you take some of those clothes off?"

"Good idea." Matt pulled his T-shirt off and tossed it over his shoulder, then shoved his shorts down. He wasn't wearing any underwear.

Chris grinned at him. "That's my little nudist."

"Hey, never say 'little' to a naked guy." Matt stretched like a cat, perfectly comfortable in nothing but skin and body jewelry.

"I see someone's ready for action." Setting the wine bottle on the windowsill, Chris slid his hands up the sides of Matt's hips, not quite touching his swelling cock. Having Rick sitting right beside him, watching him caress Matt's naked body, sent a sharp thrill through him.

"You know it, baby." Matt glanced over at Rick, who was staring at Chris's hands on him. "Touch me, Rick."

Rick's gaze darted up to meet Matt's. Licking his lips, he laid his open palm on Matt's bare hip. Matt closed his eyes.

"Mm. Feels nice." He pushed Rick's hand around to his backside. "Touch me some more, don't be shy."

Rick slid closer, pressing his body in a long line against Chris's. Chris watched, fascinated, as Rick ran one palm over the swell of Matt's butt, down the back of his thigh, up over his hip and around again to the small of his back. The sight of Rick's big hand roaming over Matt's body had Chris harder than steel, his heart racing.

"Rick," Chris said, "come here."

Rick swiveled his head around to look at Chris. They stared into each other's eyes for a heartbeat, then they were at each other like rabid dogs. Before he knew what was happening, Chris was sitting astride Rick's lap and they were grabbing at each other, hands everywhere, mouths locked together. He heard someone moaning and realized with a shock that it was him.

Fly Away

Discover the Talons Series

5 STEAMY NEW PARANORMAL ROMANCES
TO HOOK YOU IN

Kiss Me Deadly, by Shannon Stacey
King of Prey, by Mandy M. Roth
Firebird, by Jaycee Clark
Caged Desire, by Sydney Somers
Seize the Hunter, by Michelle M. Pillow

AVAILABLE IN EBOOK---COMING SOON IN PRINT!

 Samhain
Publishing ltd

WWW.SAMHAINPUBLISHING.COM

GET IT NOW

MyBookStoreAndMore.com
GREAT EBOOKS, GREAT DEALS . . . AND MORE!

Don't wait to run to the bookstore down the street, or
waste time shopping online at one of the "big boys." Now,
all your favorite Samhain authors are all in one place—at
MyBookStoreAndMore.com. Stop by today and discover
great deals on Samhain—and a whole lot more!

Samhain
Publishing Ltd

WWW.SAMHAINPUBLISHING.COM

hOt STUFF

Discover Samhain!
THE HOTTEST NEW PUBLISHER ON THE PLANET

Romance, fantasy, mystery, thriller, mainstream and
more—Samhain has more selection, hotter authors, and
everything's available in both ebook and print.

Pick your favorite, sit back, and enjoy the ride!
Hot stuff indeed.

SAMhAIN
PUbLIShING
LtD

WWW.SAMHAINPUBLISHING.COM

GREAT
Cheap
FUN

Discover eBooks!

THE FASTEST WAY TO GET THE HOTTEST NAMES

Get your favorite authors on your favorite reader, long before they're
out in print! Ebooks from Samhain go wherever you go, and work with
whatever you carry—Palm, PDF, Mobi, and more.

SAMHAIN
PUBLISHING, LTD

WWW.SAMHAINPUBLISHING.COM

Printed in the United States
103825LV00002B/127-165/A

9 781599 986418